THE COWBOY'S WAY

KATHIE DeNOSKY

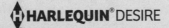

HARLEQUIN® DESIRE

Recycling programs
for this product may
not exist in your area.

ISBN-13: 978-0-373-73360-6

The Cowboy's Way

Printed in U.S.A.

"I'm not going anywhere. I want to help you out and make things easier for you and Seth."

"I don't think you being around will do anything but make things more difficult for us," she said honestly.

T.J. cupped her cheek with his palm and held her gaze with his. "There's something going on between us, Heather. I know you're as frightened for yourself by whatever it is drawing us together as you are afraid of Seth being hurt. And to tell you the truth, I'm unsettled by it, too. But I gave it a lot of thought last night and I don't think we can ignore it like it doesn't exist. I give you my word that I'll walk through hell before I hurt you or Seth."

"We can try to ignore it," she insisted, unable to sound as convincing as she would have liked. She didn't even try to deny there was a definite chemistry between them. They'd both know she was lying.

"I'm not willing to do that," he said firmly as he lowered his head.

The moment his lips settled over hers, Heather gave up trying to fight with herself...

* * *

The Cowboy's Way
is part of the #1 bestselling miniseries from
Harlequin Desire—Billionaires & Babies:
Powerful men...wrapped around their babies'
little fingers.

* * *

If you're on Twitter,
tell us what you think of Harlequin Desire!
#harlequindesire

Dear Reader,

This month I'm happy to bring you the fourth installment of The Good, The Bad and The Texan series, *The Cowboy's Way*, which is also being published as a Billionaires and Babies novel.

When T.J. Malloy first meets his neighbor, he isn't impressed. She can't seem to keep her horse on her side of the fence separating their ranches and apparently doesn't care to make the needed repairs to eliminate the problem. But when T.J. finds a woman and her young son stranded by a flooded-out road, his cowboy manners won't allow him to walk away from the situation—even if it is his nemesis, Heather Wilson. That's when he learns a valuable lesson about first impressions—sometimes things aren't always as they seem.

I hope you enjoy going along for the ride as T.J. and Heather work toward finding their happily-ever-after in *The Cowboy's Way*. Sometimes rocky, sometimes filled with unexpected detours, the road to love is never easy. But it's always worth the journey.

And as always, I hope you love reading about T.J. and Heather as much as I loved writing their story.

All the best,

Kathie DeNosky

Kathie DeNosky lives in her native southern Illinois on the land her family settled in 1839. She writes highly sensual stories with a generous amount of humor. Her books have appeared on the *USA TODAY* bestseller list and received numerous awards, including two National Readers' Choice Awards. Kathie enjoys going to rodeos, traveling to research settings for her books and listening to country music. Readers may contact her by emailing kathie@kathiedenosky.com. They can also visit her website, www.kathiedenosky.com, or find her on Facebook.

Books by Kathie DeNosky

Harlequin Desire

The Good, The Bad and The Texan series

His Marriage to Remember
A Baby Between Friends
Your Ranch...Or Mine?
The Cowboy's Way

Visit Kathie DeNosky's profile
at Harlequin.com for more titles.

This book is dedicated to all of the single parents who work so hard each and every day to meet the many challenges of raising a child alone.

One

As he sat at Sam and Bria Rafferty's dining room table after a delicious Christmas dinner prepared by his sisters-in-law, T. J. Malloy couldn't help but smile. He listened to his foster brothers and their wives talk about what they had planned for the week leading up to the family's annual New Year's Eve party, which T.J. hosted at his ranch. And, as always, there was the usual good-natured ribbing and the laughter that always followed, as well as everyone making faces and funny noises to get a smile or a giggle out of the babies. Life was good and he was one grateful son-of-a-gun for the way everything had turned out.

Thanks to their foster father, Hank Calvert, T.J. and the other five men who had been placed in the man's care when they were teenagers had straightened out their lives. In the process, they had bonded and become a family T.J. loved with all his heart. Now, he owned his own ranch, where he raised champion reining horses—a dream he'd had for most of his thirty-two years. And because he'd made several wise investments, he had more money in the bank than he could spend in three or four lifetimes.

Yup, he truly was a blessed man and he had the good sense to know it.

"Your turn, T.J.," Bria said, smiling as she dished up slices of homemade red velvet cake. "What are your plans for the week?"

"Same as every year," he said, smiling back at his sister-in-law. "I'll spend the week training my horses and waiting for you all to show up on New Year's Eve afternoon."

Four years ago when he bought the Dusty Diamond Ranch and built his seven-bedroom house, everyone had decided that he would host the family's New Year's Eve gatherings. He had enough bedrooms to accommodate the entire family, and they could all bring in the New Year together without having to be out on the roads after celebrating with a few drinks. His brothers brought their wives or a date and once the kids had been tucked in for the night, they sat around and talked or watched a movie. It had become a tradition and one that T.J. looked forward to every year.

"Do you have a lady in your life who will be joining us this year?" Nate Rafferty asked, grinning from ear to ear.

Nate and Sam were the only biological brothers of

the bunch, but they couldn't have been more different if they had tried. While Sam was a happily married family man, Nate was wilder than a range-raised colt. He loved the ladies and seemed to have made it his mission in life to date every single woman in the entire southwest. But as rowdy as he was, Nate had the same sense of loyalty that had been instilled in all of Hank's foster sons. Come hell or high water, Nate would be there for any one of them—the same as they would be there for him.

"T.J. does have a woman in his life, Nate," Lane Donaldson said, laughing as he put his arm around his wife, Taylor. "But for some reason he won't break down and ask his neighbor to join us."

"You just had to go there, didn't you, Freud?" T.J. replied, shaking his head in disgust. He should have known Lane would feel the need to comment. Having earned a master's degree in psychology, the man knew exactly which buttons to push to get a rise out of any one of them. "She and her stallion are on one side of the fence and I'm on the other. And that's the way it's going to stay."

That Wilson woman had been T.J.'s neighbor for close to two years, and he'd seen her only a handful of times. But his brothers constantly teased him about his "interest" in his ornery neighbor, even though all he knew about her was how careless she was with her horse. Hell, he didn't even know her first name. And furthermore, he didn't want to know it.

"You haven't seen her since we put up that six-foot fence between your ranch and hers this past spring?"

Sam asked, trying to dodge the glob of mashed potatoes his ten-month-old son had scooped off the high-
chair tray and tried to throw at him.

"Nope. I haven't seen her or her stallion and that
suits me just fine." T.J. couldn't help but laugh when
little Hank landed the mashed potatoes right square on
the end of Sam's nose.

"Now that you have solved the problem of her stallion jumping the fence, what are you going to complain
about?" Ryder McClain asked, laughing. His laughter
immediately turned to a groan when his baby daughter, Katie, missed the burp cloth on his shoulder and
"christened" the back of his clean shirt.

"Thank you, Katie," T.J. said, grinning as he
reached over to take the baby from his brother while
Ryder's wife, Summer, wiped off the back of his shoulder. "That shut your daddy up real quick."

"You'd better watch out, T.J.," Ryder said, grinning
back at him. "You could be next. The smell of a clean
shirt always seems to make my daughter nauseous."

The most easygoing of the band of brothers, Ryder
was also the most courageous. A rodeo bullfighter, he
used to save bull riders from serious injury, or worse,
on a regular basis. But since he'd married Summer and
they had little Katie, Ryder had cut way back on his
schedule and only worked the rodeos Nate and their
brother Jaron Lambert competed in. T.J. suspected it
was because Ryder wanted to make sure his brothers
were well protected from the dangerous bulls they rode
in their quest to become national champions. T.J. also

knew Ryder would never admit that was the reason he hadn't completely quit being a bullfighter.

"Will you be at the party, Mariah?" Lane's wife, Taylor, asked Bria's younger sister.

"Probably not," Mariah said slowly. She paused as she glanced across the table at Jaron. "I've met someone and he's asked me to go to a New Year's Eve party with him at one of the clubs up in Dallas."

Everyone looked at Jaron to see how he would react to Mariah's news. The entire family knew the two had been attracted to each other practically from the moment they'd met. But Mariah had only been eighteen at the time and at twenty-six, Jaron had decided—and rightly so—that he was too old for her. Unfortunately, in the seven years since, Jaron hadn't changed his stance and Mariah had apparently become tired of waiting on him and decided to move on.

"Congratulations on the new guy," Jaron said tightly, breaking the awkward silence. "Have a good time."

To the outward eye, his brother looked sincere, but T.J. knew better. By nature, Jaron was more reserved and quieter than the rest of the men, making it hard to figure out what he was thinking. But when he was pissed off, his voice took on an edge that was rock-hard, ice-cold and impossible to ignore. That edge was present now and T.J. knew Jaron was warning the rest of the men that he wasn't in the mood for their affectionate teasing about Mariah, now or later. T.J. also knew every one of his brothers would respect Jaron's need for silence on the matter.

"What about you, Nate?" T.J. asked, counting on the

man to ease some of the sudden tension in the room. "Are you bringing someone this year?"

Nate shook his head. "I bought the Twin Oaks Ranch over by Beaver Dam a few weeks ago," Nate stated proudly. "I've been too busy lately to think about anything but what I'm going to do with the place."

"When did this happen?" T.J. asked, astounded. "I don't recall you mentioning it when we were together at Thanksgiving."

"I didn't want to jinx it in case the deal fell through," Nate said as he shoveled a big bite of red velvet cake into his mouth.

Nate's superstition didn't surprise T.J. one bit. Every rodeo rider he knew was superstitious about something. Even he'd had certain rituals he went through before he climbed on the back of a rank bucking horse when he competed.

"You're finally putting down roots?" Sam asked, looking like he couldn't quite believe Nate was serious.

"Don't take this the wrong way, bro, but I never thought I'd see the day you settled down," Ryder said, shaking his head.

"I just bought a ranch," Nate said, grinning. "I never said I was settling down."

"When do you move into your new den of iniquity?" T.J. asked, handing baby Katie to Summer for the rest of her bottle.

"I won't be moving in for a while," Nate said, taking another bite of the red velvet cake in front of him. He shrugged. "I've got some work I need to do on it first. I'm going to knock down a couple of walls to make a great room and the plumbing and wiring need to be upgraded. I also need to make a few repairs to the fences and maybe build a couple of new barns before I bring in livestock."

"Just let us know when and how we can help and we'll be there," Lane said, speaking for all of them.

"I'll do that." Nate smiled at the women seated around the table. "And I'm counting on these lovely ladies to help out when it comes to decorating the house."

T.J. raised an eyebrow. "Even the master suite?"

Nate shook his head as his grin turned suggestive. "I've got my own ideas for that."

"I'll bet you do," Ryder said, voicing what the rest of the men were thinking.

"We can skip the details on your choice of decor for your bedroom," Bria said, handing T.J. a slice of cake.

Everyone nodded their agreement and the rest of the evening was filled with talk about renovating Nate's ranch house, causing T.J. to breathe a sigh of relief. If they were talking about something else, they weren't teasing him about his neighbor. And that was just fine with him. The less he was reminded of the woman, the better.

Several hours later, after finalizing plans for when everyone would arrive for the New Year's Eve party, T.J. left Sam and Bria's for the hour's drive back to his ranch. It had been raining all day, and by the time he reached the turn-off leading up to the Dusty Diamond's ranch house, it had become an outright downpour.

He started to turn his truck onto the lane, but then stopped when he noticed a faint glow of red about a hundred yards up ahead. The best he could tell, it was the taillights of a car and he knew without a shadow of doubt that the creek had flooded out again, blocking the road. It only happened three or four times a year, but whenever there was a significant amount of rain, the slow-moving stream that bordered his ranch to the east turned into a raging river. With as much water as had fallen over the course of the day, the creek was probably a good twenty feet or so out of its banks on either side of the ravine.

Unable to ignore the fact that whoever was in the vehicle might need help, T.J. drove on until he reached the compact gray sedan sitting in the middle of the road. He could tell someone was still inside, and from what he could see of the slim form, that someone was female. Cursing the nasty weather, T.J. got out of his truck and jogged up to the driver's side door.

"Is there anything I can do to help, ma'am?" T.J. asked as the woman inside lowered the window. She stopped halfway, and he wasn't certain if it was to keep out the rain, or because he was the one offering her assistance. But he almost groaned aloud when he realized the driver was his archenemy, that Wilson woman from the neighboring ranch.

He hadn't seen her since the last time her horse jumped the fence, back in the spring, when he'd had to take the stallion back over to the Circle W. It had been about the tenth time the horse had trespassed on Dusty Diamond land, and T.J.'s patience with the situation had come to a swift end. That's when he'd had his brothers help him put up the six-foot fence between the two properties. The fence had eliminated the problem of her horse romancing T.J.'s mares and he had thought he wouldn't have to deal with her again. Apparently, he'd been wrong.

"I was afraid of this," she said, not looking any happier to see him than he was to see her.

T.J. wasn't sure if she meant she had been afraid of not being able to get across the creek or she'd been afraid that he would be her only source of help. Either way, she wasn't in the position of being choosy, and he wouldn't walk away and leave her to solve the problem on her own. His foster father would probably come back from the dead to haunt him if Hank knew one of the boys he had raised had left a lady in distress to fend for herself.

"Even if it stops raining now, you won't be able to get back to your ranch until morning," T.J. pointed out. As he stood in the downpour, chilling water dripped off the back of his wide brimmed hat and ran down his neck. It was damned uncomfortable and he wasn't inclined to mince words. "You'll have to follow me to the Dusty Diamond. You can stay there tonight."

She stubbornly shook her head. "We may be neighbors, but I don't really know you and from our past run-ins, I'm not interested in getting acquainted."

"Believe me, lady, I'm not, either," T.J. stated flatly. "But there's no way you'll make it across forty feet of rushing water without stalling out or being swept down into the ravine. Then I'd be obligated to jump in and try to fish you out before you drowned. I'd really like to avoid that if possible." He took a deep breath and tried to hold on to his temper. "Do you have anywhere else you can go?"

As she stared at him, she caught her lower lip between her teeth as if she was trying to think of somewhere—anywhere—she could spend the night other than at his place. She finally shook her head. "No."

"Well, I'm not going to let you stay here in your car all night," he said impatiently.

"You're not going to *let* me stay in my car?"

From the tone of her voice, he could tell he had ruffled more than a couple of feathers.

"Look, I'm just trying to keep you from having to spend a damp, uncomfortable night in your car," he stated. "But it's your choice. If you want to sit out here instead of sleeping in a warm, dry bed, that's your choice."

When it dawned on him that she might be frightened of him, he felt a little guilty for being so blunt. He could even understand her reluctance to take him up on his offer. The few times they had come face-to-face, he had been angry. She probably thought he was an ill-tempered bastard. Unfortunately, he wasn't doing anything now to correct that impression.

"Hey, I'm sorry," he said, making a conscious effort to remove the impatience from his tone. "It's dark, cold and I'm getting soaked to the bone out here." He hoped the friendly smile he gave her helped to alleviate some of her fears. "It's warm and dry at my place and I've got plenty of room." As an afterthought, he added, "And all of the bedrooms have locks on the doors."

She glanced in the rearview mirror at something

in the backseat, then hesitated a few seconds longer before she shook her head. She sounded tired and utterly defeated when she finally murmured, "I don't have a choice."

"When we get to the house, you can park in the garage," he offered. "There's plenty of room and you'll be able to stay dry getting inside the house."

"All right. I'll follow you," she said, rolling up the driver's side window.

He jogged back to his truck and started it up. Once he had it turned around and checked to make sure she wasn't having any trouble doing the same, T.J. drove back to the lane leading up to his home. When he steered the truck around the ranch house to the attached three-car garage, he pressed the remote to raise two of the wide doors and parked inside. By the time he got out, the woman had stopped her older Toyota between his truck and the Mercedes sedan he rarely drove.

He walked over and opened her door. When she got out of the car, his breath caught. The times he had taken her errant horse back to her and knocked on her door to demand she keep the horse on her ranch, as well as during their conversation a few minutes ago in the dark, cold rain, he had been so frustrated, he hadn't paid much attention to his neighbor's looks. But he sure as hell noticed them now.

A few inches over six feet tall, T.J. didn't meet many women who could look him square in the eye without having to tilt their heads back. But the Wilson woman was only four or five inches shorter than him. When their gazes met, he felt like he had been kicked in the gut.

She had the bluest eyes he'd ever seen and for reasons that baffled him, he wanted to take her long, strawberry blond hair down from her ponytail and run his fingers through the soft-looking, wavy strands. The woman wasn't just pretty, she was heart-stoppingly gorgeous. He couldn't believe he had missed seeing that before.

When she turned to open the back door of her car and reached inside, he briefly wondered if she carried an overnight bag around just on the outside chance she got stranded somewhere. But when she straightened and turned to face him, T.J. barely managed to keep his jaw from dropping. She held a blanket-covered child to her shoulder with one arm, while she tried to keep her grasp on her purse and a diaper bag with the other.

In the course of about three seconds several questions ran through his mind. First, he remembered that when he'd stopped to see if she needed help, she had been sitting in her car contemplating how she was going to get back to her ranch. Surely she wouldn't have tried to cross the flooded road with her kid in the backseat? The realization of what might have happened if she had tried such a thing caused a tight knot to form in the pit of his stomach. Second, when he'd asked her if there was anywhere else she could go, she had told him there wasn't. What would she have done if he hadn't come along and offered her shelter for the night? Would she have tried to tough it out all night in the car with a child?

"Let me help you," T.J. said now, stepping forward to take her purse and the diaper bag. Aside from the fact that it was just good manners for a man to help a woman carry things, the dark smudges beneath her eyes were testament to the fact that she was extremely tired.

"Thank you...Malloy." She shook her head as she closed the car door. "I don't know your first name."

When he stepped back for her to precede him through the door leading into the mudroom, he did his best to give her a friendly smile. "The name's T.J., Ms. Wilson."

He suddenly realized that in the four years since he'd bought the ranch, he'd been so busy starting his breeding program and getting settled in, that he hadn't bothered to get acquainted with more than one or two of the other ranchers in the immediate area. And the few times he had met up with Ms. Wilson, it hadn't been under the best of circumstances. He had been pissed off about her stallion impregnating his mares and hadn't bothered to introduce himself and, understandably, she hadn't been inclined to give him her name or exchange pleasantries when he had put her on the defensive.

He felt a little guilty about that. Oh, who was he kidding? He felt downright ashamed of himself. No matter if he had been angry or not, he had better manners than that and shouldn't have been so demanding.

"My name's Heather," she said as they walked into the kitchen. When he turned on the lights, she stopped and looked around. "Your home is very nice."

"Thanks." He set her purse and the diaper bag on the kitchen island, then shrugged out of his wet jacket before helping her out of hers. "Would you like something to eat or drink, Heather?" he asked, doing his best to be cordial.

"Thank you, but it's late and if you don't mind, I'd rather get my son settled down for the night," she said, sounding as if she was ready to drop in her tracks.

"No problem." Hanging their coats in the mudroom, he picked up the two bags and led the way down the hall to the stairs in the foyer. "Do you need to call someone to let them know where you are and that you and your little boy are all right?"

T.J. wondered where her significant other was and why he wasn't with her. Any man worth a damn wouldn't have let his woman go out alone on a night like this. In T.J.'s opinion, there was no excuse for the man not being on the cell phone at that very moment checking to see that she and their little boy were safe and going to be all right.

Climbing the steps, she shook her head. "No. There's no one. It's just me and Seth."

When T.J. stopped and opened the door to the first bedroom on the second floor, he stepped back for her to enter. "Ladies first." Following her into the room, he added, "If this isn't to your liking, I've got five more bedrooms to choose from."

"This is fine, thank you," she said, reaching for her purse and the diaper bag as if she would like for him to leave.

When her hand brushed his, he felt a tingling sensation along his skin and quickly reasoned that it was probably a charge of static electricity. But he couldn't dismiss the heat he felt radiating from her quite so easily.

Frowning, he asked, "Are you feeling all right?"

"I've felt better," she admitted as she set the two bags on the bench at the end of the bed.

Without a second thought about the invasion of her space, T.J. walked over and placed his palm on her forehead. "You've got a fever." Lifting the edge of the blanket, he noticed the sleeping baby's flushed cheeks. "Both of you are sick."

"We'll be fine," she said, placing the little boy on the bed. "I had to take my son to the emergency room. I was on my way back home when you stopped to see if we needed help."

"What was the diagnosis?" T.J. asked, hoping the little guy was going to be okay.

"He has an ear infection." She reached for the diaper bag. "They gave me an antibiotic for him, as well as something to give him if his fever spikes."

"What about you?" he asked. "Did you see a doctor while you were there?"

She shook her head. "I'll be all right. I'm just getting over the flu."

"You should have seen a doctor as well," he said, unable to keep the disapproval from his voice.

"Well, I didn't," she retorted as if she resented his observation. "Now, if you'll excuse me—"

"While you get him settled in bed, I'll go get something for you to sleep in," he interrupted, leaving the room before she could protest.

When he entered the master suite, T.J. walked straight to the medicine cabinet in his adjoining bathroom. Taking a bottle of Tylenol from one of the shelves, he went back into his bedroom and looked around. What could he give her to wear to bed? He preferred sleeping in the buff and didn't even own a pair of pajamas. Deciding that one of his flannel shirts would have to do, he took one from the walk-in closet and headed back to the room Heather and her son would be using.

"Will this be okay?" he asked, holding up the soft shirt for her inspection. "I'm sorry I don't have something more comfortable."

"I could have just slept in my clothes," she said, covering the baby with the comforter. Turning to face him, she took the garment he offered. "But thank you for…everything."

"Here's something to take for your fever," he said, handing her the bottle of Tylenol. He went into the adjoining bathroom for a glass of water, then handed it to her as he pointed to the bottle. "Take a couple of these and if you need anything else, my room is down at the other end of the hall."

"We'll be fine," she said, removing two of the tablets from the bottle.

He stared at her for a moment, wondering for the second time since finding her stranded on the road how he could have missed how beautiful she was all those times he took her horse back to her. Even with dark smudges under her eyes, she was striking and the kind of woman a man couldn't help but wonder—

"Was there something else?" she asked, snapping him back to reality.

Deciding the rain must have washed away some of his good sense, he shook his head. "Good night."

When he left the room and closed the door, he heard the quiet snick of the lock being set behind him as he started down the hall to his bedroom. Under the circumstances, he could understand her caution. A woman alone couldn't be too careful these days. She didn't know him and until tonight, he hadn't given her a reason to think she might want to change that fact.

"You're one sorry excuse for a man," he muttered to himself.

He'd had his mind made up that she was just a defiant, uncaring female who arrogantly ignored his pleas to keep her horse at home. It had never occurred to him that she was every bit as vulnerable and overworked as any other single mother. Of course, he hadn't known about the kid until tonight. But that was no excuse for jumping to conclusions about her the way he had.

As T.J. took off his damp clothes and headed for the shower to wash away the uncomfortable chill of the cold rain, he couldn't stop thinking about his guests down the hall. He didn't know what the story was with Heather and her little boy, but it really didn't matter. Whether she wanted to accept his help or not, right now she needed it. She and her kid were both sick, and since there didn't seem to be anyone else to see to their welfare, T.J. was going to have to step up to the plate.

One of the first things Hank Calvert had taught him and his brothers was that when they saw someone in need, it was only right to pitch in and lend a hand. He had told them that life could be an obstacle and sometimes it took teamwork to get through it. And if anyone ever needed a helping hand it was Heather Wilson.

Of course, T.J. didn't think Hank had ever run into anyone with as much stubborn pride as Heather. The woman wore that pride like a suit of armor and was a little too independent for her own good. He toweled himself dry, walked into the bedroom and got into bed. He lay there for several long minutes, staring up at the ceiling as he listened to the rain pelt the roof. Heather's situation was a lot like his own mother's.

Delia Malloy had been a single mother with all the responsibilities that entailed. She had done a great job of holding down a job and providing for their family of two while she raised him. T.J. would always be grateful for the sacrifices she had made. But when he was ten years old, they both came down with the flu. That was when his life changed forever.

His mother had taken good care of him and made sure he recovered with no problems, but what she hadn't done was take care of herself. Physically rundown, she developed a case of pneumonia and hadn't been able to fight off the infection. She died a week later and T.J. had been sent to live with his elderly great-grandmother.

That's when all hell broke loose and started him on a downward spiral that ended up sending him to the Last Chance Ranch. His great-grandmother had really been too old to oversee what he was up to and who he was with. And he had been too hurt and angry about losing his mother to listen to her anyway. Looking back, he had been ripe for falling in with the wrong crowd and by the time he was thirteen, he had been arrested five times for vandalism and criminal mischief. Shortly after that his great-grandmother passed away and his case worker had decided that placing him with a set of normal foster parents would be more of the same, so he had been placed under the care of Hank Calvert. And even though it had been the luckiest break of his life, he was determined to see that Heather's little boy didn't go down the same path he had taken.

Her little boy was counting on his mother to be there for him throughout the rest of his childhood, and for the kid's sake, T.J. would try to make sure that happened— at least this time. Whether she liked it or not, he was going to take care of Heather and her son while they were sick and flooded out of returning to their home. In the bargain, he'd make sure that her little boy didn't suffer the same motherless childhood that T.J. had.

Around dawn the morning after she followed T.J. Malloy home, Heather lay in bed, feeling as if she had been run over by a truck. Assessing her symptoms, she realized that although her muscles weren't as achy as they had been for the past couple of days, they were extremely weak. Just lifting her head from the pillow took monumental effort. Thankfully her headache was gone, but one minute she was hot and the next she was shivering—indicating that her temperature was still elevated. Thank heavens she had been able to scrape up the money to get Seth to the doctor a couple of months earlier for a flu shot. At least she wouldn't have to worry about him catching the illness from her.

"Mom-mom," Seth said, sitting up to pat her arm.

She could tell from the tremor in his voice that he was about to cry and she knew why. For an almost two-year-old, he was a sound sleeper and had slept through the night since he was three months old. But he wasn't used to sleeping anywhere but his own bed, in his own room, and he was probably disoriented by the strange surroundings.

"It's all right, sweetie."

Rubbing his back, she hoped he would settle back down and sleep for a little while longer before he insisted they get up for breakfast. Since coming down with the flu, it had been a real struggle to take care of a toddler, as well as a barn full of horses by herself, and she couldn't help but want to get a little more sleep while she could. Fortunately, it had been a mild case of the illness or she would have never been able to manage on her own. But without being able to get enough rest, it was taking her twice as long to get over it.

Just as Seth closed his eyes and seemed to be drifting back to sleep, a tap on the door caused him to jerk awake and start to cry.

Shivering from the chills and feeling as if her legs were made of lead, Heather picked up her crying son and got out of bed. Without thinking about the fact that she was wearing nothing more than Malloy's flannel shirt and her panties, she walked over to unlock and open the door. "What?"

"I thought you and your little boy might like something to eat," Malloy said, holding out a tray of food.

If she had felt better, she might have tried not to sound so impatient. She might have acknowledged his thoughtfulness. At the moment, just the thought of food made her stomach queasy and she wished he hadn't disturbed her son.

"Th-thank you, but..." Her voice trailed off when she noticed his expression. "Is s-something wrong?"

"Let me help you back to bed," he said, brushing past her to set the tray on the dresser. "I'd ask if you still have a fever, but I already know the answer."

"H-how?" She wished her teeth would stop chattering like a cheap pair of castanets.

Turning back, he took Seth from her, then put his arm around her shoulders and guided her back to the bed. "Just a hunch," he answered, smiling.

Once she was back in bed, she noticed that Seth had stopped crying and was staring at the tray of food Malloy had set on the dresser. "Mom-mom, eat."

Groaning, she started to get up, but Malloy stopped her. "I'm assuming that means he's hungry?" When she nodded, he pointed to the tray. "I've got toast and scrambled eggs. Do you think he'll let me feed him while you rest?"

She barely managed to nod before she pulled the comforter around herself and closed her eyes. If she felt better, she would have asked why he was being so nice to her, instead of thinking about how handsome he was. Her breath caught. Where had that come from?

If she was thinking T. J. Malloy was good-looking, her fever had to have made her delirious. That was the only explanation. If she could just rest for a moment, she'd be able to get up and take over feeding her son, as well as return to her senses.

Two

When Heather opened her eyes again, she noticed that the sun was shining through a part in the curtain and Seth was sound asleep on the bed beside her. Looking a little closer, she noticed he was wearing a pair of pajamas she had never seen before and his copper-red hair had been neatly combed to the side.

How long had she been asleep and where had the clothes her son was wearing come from?

Glancing at the clock on the nightstand, Heather couldn't believe that it was already midafternoon. She had slept for eight straight hours. She couldn't remember getting that much sleep at one stretch since before Seth was born.

Her heart stalled. Had T. J. Malloy taken care of her son?

She vaguely remembered a knock waking Seth and her opening the door to find Malloy standing on the other side with a tray of food. Had she dreamed that he had helped her back to bed?

When she realized that all she had on was his shirt and her panties, Heather closed her eyes and hoped when she opened them she would somehow be transported to her own bed in the Circle W ranch house and that the past twenty-four hours would prove to be nothing more than a dream. But aside from her embarrassment over a stranger seeing her wearing so little, she wasn't entirely comfortable with the fact that Malloy had taken care of Seth. She didn't really know her neighbor and from the previous run-ins she'd had with him, she wasn't sure he was someone she wanted around her son. When Malloy had brought her stallion back the few times Magic Dancer had jumped the fence between their properties, the man had been the biggest grouch she had ever met.

"The horses," she murmured suddenly, remembering that she had livestock to feed. Hopefully the water blocking the road had receded. She needed to get home to tend to the horses, as well as make sure the buckets she had left in the utility room to catch the drips from the leaking roof hadn't overflowed.

As she sat up, Heather realized she felt a lot better than she had that morning. Her fever was gone. Maybe she had turned the corner and was over the worst of the flu. Sleeping all night and most of the day had probably been a tremendous help. It was a shame she hadn't had the opportunity when she'd first come down with the illness. Her recovery time would have been a lot shorter.

But she hadn't had that luxury in so long, it was hard to remember what it was like to have help with anything. After she had Seth, she'd had no choice but to let go of the men who had worked for her late father because she couldn't afford to pay them. It was the only way she had been able to make ends meet on the Circle W. That meant she had to take care of feeding the horses, mucking out stalls and trying to keep up the endless other chores on a working horse ranch, as well as take care of a baby.

Careful not to wake Seth, she started to get up, then immediately sat back down on the side of the bed when her knees began to shake. She might be feeling better, but she was still extremely weak. It was going to be a real test of her fortitude to lift heavy buckets of water and bales of hay while she was in this state.

She tried again, and had just managed to walk over to the rocking chair where she had draped her clothes the night before, when the door opened.

"You shouldn't be up yet," Malloy said, entering the room and walking over to her.

She supposed he had the right to just waltz right in without asking if she minded. After all, he did own the place. But she wasn't happy about it.

She grabbed her jeans and sweatshirt and held them in front of her. "Don't you believe in knocking?"

"I was just checking on your little boy and didn't expect you to be awake yet." He shrugged as if he wasn't the least bit concerned about it. "How are you feeling?"

"I'm much better and as soon as I get dressed, Seth and I will go home and leave you alone." She wished he would leave the room so she could take a quick shower before Seth woke up.

"Don't worry about getting back home," he said, his deep voice wrapping around her like a comforting cloak. "You really should stay until there's no danger of a setback."

Heather shook her head as much to stop the lulling effect of his voice as in refusal. "I appreciate everything you've done, but I don't want to impose." Feeling her knees start to shake again, she sat down on the rocking chair. "Besides, I need to get my livestock fed."

"All you have to do is rest and get better," he said, smiling. "I had one of my crew go over to your place when the water receded around noon to let your men know you and the little guy were okay. Since no one was around, my man took care of feeding your horses for you."

She looked up at him and was hit with an unexpected observation. T. J. Malloy wasn't just handsome, he was knock-your-socks-off good-looking. Her breath caught.

The few times that he had brought her horse home, she hadn't noticed anything beyond his dark scowl and formidable stance as he threatened to take legal action against her if she didn't keep her horse on her side of the fence. But without his wide-brimmed, black Resistol pulled down low on his brow, she could see a kindness in his striking hazel eyes that she would never have expected. And for some reason she found his brown hair, which curled around his ears and over the nape of his neck, sexy and rather endearing.

She frowned. Where had that come from? And why did she find anything about the man attractive?

It had to be some kind of residual effect of the fever. It was causing her to see Malloy in a different light. Surely as soon as she recovered her strength, she would come to her senses, regain her perspective and see that T. J. Malloy was just as unpleasant and unappealing as ever.

"Are you feeling all right?" he asked, looking concerned.

"Uh, yes," she said, nodding. "I'm just a little weak." As an afterthought, she added, "Thank you for having one of your hired hands tend to my horses."

"No problem." He gave her the same smile that had caused the illusion of him being amiable. "I assume you gave your men the rest of the holiday weekend off?"

"Since you sent one of yours over to take care of my horses, I assume you didn't?" she asked instead of answering his question.

She didn't want to tell him that she'd had to lay off the two men. For one thing, it was a matter of pride. She didn't want Malloy realizing that the Circle W had fallen on such hard times. And for another, she didn't like anyone knowing that she and her child lived alone on the ranch. Not that it made a lot of difference, but she felt a little safer with people thinking the hired men were still in residence.

"I did offer to let them off, but they preferred me paying them double time for working this weekend," he said, unaware of her thoughts. "So don't worry about the horses until your men get back on Monday. I'll have one of mine go over there again tomorrow and Sunday to take care of them."

"That isn't necessary," she insisted. "I'll do it."

He stubbornly folded his arms across his broad chest and shook his head. "You need to take it easy for a couple more days and make sure you're completely over the flu before you start doing anything too strenuous. You won't be doing yourself or your little boy any favors if you're in the hospital with pneumonia." Something in his tone, as well as his body language, told her than he was determined to have his way in the matter.

Just as determined to have her own way, she shook her head. "Don't worry about me. I'll be fine."

"That's what you said last night and this morning," he remarked. "I wouldn't consider barely having enough strength to stand doing all that great."

He probably had a point, but she hated to admit that he was right, almost as much as she hated that she found him so darned good-looking.

"Why do you care?" she asked bluntly. Apparently the flu had removed some kind of filter in her brain. She was unable to keep from blurting out whatever she was thinking.

His easy expression changed to the dark scowl she was more used to seeing from him. "Having the flu isn't something you should take lightly. It can have serious complications. I'm just trying to make sure you're around to raise your little boy, lady."

She knew he was only doing what he thought was

right, but it had been a very long time since anyone had cared to lend her their assistance or show they were concerned for her well-being. Even her late fiancé's parents had severed all ties with her when their son died. And they hadn't bothered contacting her since, even knowing she had been pregnant with their grandchild. That's when she had decided she didn't need them or anyone else. She was a strong, capable woman and could do whatever had to be done on her own.

Shrugging, she stared down at the clothes in her lap. "I'm sorry if I sound ungrateful," she said, meaning it. "There's no excuse for my being rude. I do appreciate your help. But I've taken care of Seth since I came down with the flu and I'm doing a lot better now. I know I'll be fine." She looked up into his hazel eyes. "Really."

"I respect your need for independence," he said, his tone less harsh. "All I'm trying to do is help you out for a couple more days. Rest up here, at least until tomorrow. I'll have one of my men go over to your place, then all you'll have to do when you get home is take care of yourself and your little boy."

It was obvious he wasn't going to give up and she wasn't up to a full-scale verbal battle. And honestly, it would be nice to not have to take on everything all by herself for once.

"All right," she finally conceded. "One of your men can take care of the horses for me tomorrow, but now that the road is clear there's no reason for us to stay here and inconvenience you any longer." She pointed toward the bathroom door. "Now if you'll excuse me,

I'd like to take a shower and get dressed so we can go on home. Seth and I have taken up enough of your time and generosity. Besides, we'll both rest better in our own beds."

She could tell Malloy wanted to say something about her insistence on going home, but Seth chose that moment to rouse up and start crying. Normally a sound sleeper, he could snooze through just about anything at home. But now that he was unfamiliar with the surroundings, their arguing had obviously disturbed him.

"It's all right, sweetie," she said, getting out of the chair. When she walked over to the bed to pick him up, she discovered that it took more effort than usual.

"Here, let me help," Malloy said, stepping forward to pick up her son.

To her surprise when Seth recognized who held him, the little traitor laid his head on the man's shoulder and smiled at her.

"Did you give him his medication?" she asked, feeling like a complete failure as a mother. She had slept while a total stranger fed, changed and apparently bonded with her child.

Malloy nodded. "I read the dosage on the bottle's label and gave the antibiotic to him right after breakfast and then again after lunch."

"You seem to know a lot about taking care of a child," she commented, wondering if he might have one of his own. She felt a little let down that he might have a significant other somewhere, but she couldn't for the life of her figure out why.

"I have a ten-month-old nephew and a six-month-old niece," he answered, as if reading her mind. "But other than watching their parents take care of them, I'm a trial-and-error kind of guy. That's why I had to change this little guy's sleeper and my shirt after lunch." Malloy grinned. "I *tried* to let him feed himself and quickly learned that was an *error*."

Heather smiled at the visual image as an unfamiliar emotion spread throughout her chest. There was something about a man being unafraid to hold and nurture a child that was heartwarming.

Not at all comfortable with the fact that the man drawing that emotion from her was T. J. Malloy, she asked, "Would you mind watching him for a few minutes while I take a quick shower?"

"Not at all," he said, shaking his head. "Take your time. You'll probably feel a lot better."

"I'll feel better when we get home." She stared down at the jeans and sweatshirt she still held. "Seth is going to need diapers and we both need clean clothes."

"Not a problem," Malloy answered. "I had one of my men drive up to Stephenville this morning to pick up a few things I thought you would need. I had him get both of you a change of clothes, as well as diapers and some kind of little kid food."

"How did he know what sizes to get?" That explained where Seth's new pajamas came from.

"I told Dan to take his wife along for the ride." Malloy looked quite pleased with himself. "They have three kids under the age of five and I figured if anyone would know what you both needed, it would be Jane Ann."

He pointed toward the dresser. "Your clothes are over there in the shopping bag."

"I'll reimburse you for everything," she said, thankful to have clean clothes to put on after her shower. "Do you still have the sales slip?"

"No, I don't and no, you won't pay me back," he said, firmly.

"Yes, I will." She didn't have a lot in reserve and hoped it didn't cost much, but she did have her pride. She wasn't the gold digger her fiancé's parents had once accused her of being when she'd called to let them know about Seth's birth. And besides, considering her past with Malloy, she wasn't inclined to have him complaining about some other way she'd been negligent.

Malloy released a frustrated sigh. "We'll discuss it later."

"You can bet we will," she vowed.

Deciding there was no reasoning with the man at the moment, Heather tugged at the shirt she was wearing to make sure it covered her backside as she got the bag of clothes from the dresser, then walked into the bathroom and shut the door.

When she looked in the mirror, she groaned. Her long hair resembled a limp mop and other than the few freckles sprinkled across her nose and cheekbones, she was the color of a ghost—and a sickly one at that.

But as she continued to stare in the mirror, the weight of reality began to settle across her shoulders like a leaden yoke. A shower and clean clothes could make her feel a little better physically and T. J. Malloy could offer as much neighborly help as he wanted, but nothing could wash away the worry or the hopelessness she faced when she returned home.

Unless something miraculous happened between now and the end of the January, she and her son were going to be homeless. And there didn't seem to be a thing she could do to stop it from happening.

When Heather went into the adjoining bathroom and closed the door, T.J. sat down on the rocking chair with Seth and released the breath he had been holding.

What the hell was wrong with him? The woman looked thoroughly exhausted, was just getting over the flu and, without a shadow of doubt, was as irritable as a bull in a herd full of steers. So why was he thinking about how sexy she looked wearing his shirt? Or how long and shapely her legs were?

Earlier that morning, he had damned near dropped the breakfast tray he had been carrying when she opened the door. She hadn't bothered with the top couple of buttons on the flannel shirt he'd given her to sleep in and he'd noticed the valley between her breasts. What was worse, she had been too ill to even try to be enticing and she had still managed to tie him into a knot the size of his fist.

"You're one sick SOB, Malloy," he muttered, shaking his head.

As he sat there trying to figure out what it was about her that he found so damned alluring, he frowned. He wanted her out of his hair as much as she wanted to leave. So why did he keep insisting that Heather needed to stay another night? Why couldn't he keep his mouth shut, help her get her son buckled into his car seat and wave goodbye as they drove away?

Looking down at the little boy sitting on his lap, T.J. shook his head. "Be glad you're too young to notice anything about girls. They'll make you completely crazy with little or no effort."

When Seth looked up at him and grinned, T.J. suddenly knew exactly why he was being overly cautious about them leaving. He couldn't stop comparing Seth's situation with T.J.'s own as a kid. Every child deserved to have their mother with them for as long as possible, and although Heather was clearly over the worst of her illness and thought she was ready to go home, he wanted to make sure there was no possibility of a serious complication. If she had her hands full taking care of a kid and a ranch while she continued to recover that would increase the chances of her having a relapse—or worse.

"I'm just trying to keep your momma upright and mobile for you, little guy," T.J. said, smiling back at the child.

The little copper-haired boy on his lap gave him a big grin and patted T.J.'s cheek as he babbled something T.J. didn't understand. He figured Seth was thanking him for taking care of his mother and an unfamiliar tightening filled T.J.'s chest. As kids went, Heather's was awesome. Friendly and well-behaved, Seth was no problem to watch and if he ever had a kid, T.J. wanted one just like him.

He gave Seth a hug. "I'll make sure to see that you're

both taken care of so that you can be together a long time."

He had a sneaking suspicion there was more to his interference than that, but he wasn't going to delve too deeply into his own motivation. He wasn't sure he would be overly comfortable with what he discovered. Hell, he still wasn't comfortable with the fact that he found his nemesis even remotely attractive.

The sudden crack of thunder followed closely by the sound of rain beating hard against the roof caused T.J.'s smile to turn into an outright grin. "It looks like Mother Nature agrees with me about the two of you staying put," he said, drawing a giggle from Seth.

A few minutes later, when Heather walked back into the bedroom after her shower, T.J. noticed she wore the new set of gray sweats Jane Ann had picked out for her. He wouldn't have thought it was possible, but damned if the woman didn't manage to make baggy fleece look good.

His lower body twitched and he had to swallow around the cotton coating his throat. Heather was as prickly as a cactus patch and tried to reject everything he did to help her, but that didn't keep him from wanting to take her in his arms and kiss her senseless.

Unsettled by the wayward thought, he focused on telling her about how the nasty weather would change her plans. "You don't have a choice now. You're going to have to stay here until tomorrow."

Her vivid blue eyes narrowed. "Are you telling me that you won't allow me to leave?"

"Nope. I'm not telling you anything of the sort,"

he said, quickly deciding that he needed to watch the way he phrased things. He had seen that warning look in his sisters-in-law's eyes when his brothers made a verbal blunder and he wasn't fool enough to ignore it. "I'm just making an observation."

Heather frowned. "Would you care to explain that?"

"Listen." He pointed toward the ceiling and knew the moment the sound of rain pounding on the roof registered with her from the defeated expression on her face. "It's coming down like somebody's pouring it out of a bucket. With as much rain as we had yesterday, the creek is full and it's a good bet the road is already starting to flood again."

Groaning, she sank down on the side of the bed. "I have things I need to do at home."

T.J. shrugged. "The livestock are already taken care of. I'm sure whatever else there is you need to tend to will keep until tomorrow."

As soon as the words were out, he could tell he had pissed her off again. "Do you dismiss what you need to get done as unimportant?" she asked, spearing him with her sharp blue gaze.

"It depends," he answered, wondering why she had taken offense to his comment and why he found her spitfire temper a little exciting. "If it needs my attention right away, I take care of it."

"Then what makes you think the things I need to get done are different?" She stood up to fold the clothes she had worn the day before and stuffed them into the shopping bag. "You don't have any idea what I have to do or what might need my immediate attention."

He felt as if he had stepped into a minefield—any way he went could prove explosive. "I didn't mean to imply that your concerns are less important than mine." Suddenly irritated with her short temper, he set her little boy on his feet and watched Seth walk over to his mother, then he rose from the rocking chair. "I just meant that whatever you need to do will have to wait until after the water recedes again. And before this escalates into something that could make the remainder of your stay a pain in my..." Pausing, he looked down at the toddler gazing up at him. He wasn't about to add a word to the kid's vocabulary that she could take him to task over. "Make the remainder of your stay difficult, I think I'll go see what I can rustle up for our supper." Walking out into the hall, he turned back. "I'll be up later to help you and Seth downstairs. And don't even think about trying it on your own. A broken neck won't help you get away from here any faster."

Before she had a chance to tie into him over something else, he closed the door. He descended the stairs and went into the kitchen to see what he could find for them to eat.

"So much for trying to be a nice guy," he muttered as he opened the refrigerator to remove packages of deli meats and condiments. Slamming the food down onto the kitchen island, he turned to get a loaf of bread from the bread box on the counter. "If she fell down the stairs she'd probably find a way to blame me and then sue my ass off."

"Do you need me to help with dinner, Malloy?"

When he turned back, Heather and her son stood

just inside the doorway. Closing his eyes for a moment, T.J. tried to shore up his patience.

"You didn't listen to a dam...dang thing I said, did you?" he asked, opening his eyes to look directly at her. "As weak as you are you shouldn't have tried the stairs on your own. Did you even consider that you or your little boy could have fallen and been seriously hurt?"

"I'm not a hothouse flower. I can do things on my own. I *have* been doing things on my own. Besides, we took it slow and I held on to the railing," she said, shrugging one slender shoulder. "As you can see, Seth and I made it to the bottom without incident."

He shook his head at her stubbornness. "Do me a favor and don't try it on your own again. I'd rather you didn't tempt fate."

"I'll think about it." She was silent for a minute before she asked bluntly, "Why are you being so nice to me and my son? Why do you care what happens to us?"

T.J. stared at her for a moment. He supposed he could understand her wariness. Before last night the only times she had seen him were under less than favorable circumstances. He had been returning her errant stallion—the one who had covered his mares and ruined his breeding program for more than a year—and hadn't really cared to be overly polite.

"I think before we go any further, I need to explain something," he said seriously. "All those times I had to bring your horse back to you, I was angry that he'd covered several of my mares. I raise and train reining horses and having them bred by a rogue stallion set my breeding program back by at least a year." He shook his head. "But I could have been more civil when I asked you to keep him confined, instead of making demands and threatening to get the law involved."

She stared at him for several long moments and just when he thought she was going to reject his apology and explanation, she nodded. "I can understand your frustration and I'm sorry about him causing a delay in your breeding program. I did try to keep him on the Circle W, but I think Magic tries to live up to his name. He can be a regular Houdini when it comes to getting out of his stall or around a fence."

"Some horses are like that," T.J. admitted. "Especially studs when there's a harem of mares waiting for them."

They were both silent for several long seconds before she spoke again. "As long as we're clearing the air, I owe you another apology. You've been very accommodating and I really do appreciate all of your help. Earlier I was frustrated that Seth and I weren't going to be able to go home, but that's no excuse for taking it out on you. I'm sorry."

"I'll accept your apology if you'll accept mine," he said, meaning it. "I should have been more understanding about your horse getting out."

A hint of a smile appeared as she led her little boy over to the opposite side of the kitchen island, where T.J. stood. "And just to put your mind at ease, if I had fallen down the stairs, I wouldn't have sued you, Malloy."

He couldn't help but grin as he opened one of the cabinets above the counter and reached for a couple of sandwich plates. "The name's T.J. and I'm glad I won't have to be calling my lawyer." As he started making their sandwiches, he added, "So what do you say we start over and try being a little more neighborly with each other from now on?"

When he noticed the twinkle in her blue eyes and the dimples on either side of her mouth as she smiled at him, he felt like he'd taken a sucker punch to the gut. He had to have been as blind as a damned bat not to have noticed how pretty she was before.

"I suppose being more congenial is better than wanting to shoot you on sight," she said, oblivious to his thoughts.

T.J. laughed, releasing some of the tension suddenly gripping him. "Yeah, being friendly is preferable to dodging lead." He pointed to the slices of meat and cheese in front of him. "My housekeeper is up in Dallas with her family until after the first of the year and I'm not very good at cooking. I hope you don't mind sandwiches for supper."

"A sandwich is fine for me." She shook her head. "I still don't have much of an appetite anyway. But if you don't mind, I'd like to find something else for Seth. I try to make sure he gets his veggies every day."

"When I sent Dan and his wife to Stephenville, Jane Ann got a few frozen dinners she said were especially for little kids." T.J. nodded toward the refrigerator. "She said they weren't her first choice for feeding toddlers, but they would be better for Seth than some of the things I'd probably try to feed him." He couldn't help but laugh. "I zapped one of them in the microwave for lunch and I can honestly say, he really enjoyed fling-ing the macaroni and mini meatballs at me."

"He behaves pretty well for being almost two, but he still has his moments," she said, laughing as she and the kid walked over to open the freezer door on the side-by-side refrigerator.

The sound of Heather's laughter caused a warm feel-ing to spread throughout his chest. He didn't have a clue why, but for some reason it felt good to make her laugh.

T.J. frowned as he finished the sandwiches and set them on the table. He and Heather were little more than strangers and he still wasn't convinced they could be friends. Why did he care one way or the other that he had made her laugh?

He wasn't sure what his problem was, but he decided that some things were better left unexplored. He was al-ready having enough trouble with the fact that Heather and her son hadn't been on the Dusty Diamond a full twenty-four hours and he'd noticed—even when she was at her worst with the flu and wearing a baggy set of sweats—that she was sexy as sin. If that wasn't proof enough that he was one extremely disturbed hombre, he didn't know what was.

"This is a very interesting family room," Heather said when T.J. showed her and Seth around his house after they finished dinner. "But I think this would come closer to qualifying as a man cave than a place where a family gathers."

He chuckled. "That's what I usually call it, but I

thought it might sound a little more inviting if I referred to it as the family room."

One wall of the huge space was dominated by an antique bar that looked as if it had come straight from a saloon in an old Western movie. Made of dark mahogany, the intricate carvings on the front were complemented by the marble inlayed top and the highly polished brass boot rail attached along the bottom a few inches above the floor. A large mirror in an ornate gold frame hung on the wall behind the bar Shelves on both sides were filled with expensive-looking whiskey, rum and tequila bottles. Several feet from the end of the bar an old-fashioned billiard table with hand-tied leather strip pockets stood, waiting for someone to send the racked, brightly colored balls rolling across its green felt top. All that was missing from that side of the room was a saloon girl with rosy red rouge on her cheeks and a come-hither look in her eyes.

"Would you like to watch a movie?" he asked, motioning toward the biggest flat-screen television she had ever seen. It graced the wall at the far end of the room. It wasn't surprising to see that speakers had been hung on the walls surrounding the area, guaranteeing the viewer an audio experience that was sure to make him or her feel as if they were part of the action.

"I've got all the satellite movie channels, as well as pay-per-view," he added. "I'm sure we could find something to watch that you'd like."

The huge, comfortable-looking, brown leather sectional sofa in front of the television looked extremely inviting and Heather was tempted. "Maybe another time," she said, hiding a yawn behind her hand. "I'm afraid I'm still pretty tired and it won't be long before I'll have to get Seth in bed for the night."

"It's understandable that you're tired. You haven't regained all of your strength." When Seth walked past him toward a basket of toys beside the sofa, T.J. grinned. "And before you ask if those are mine, I keep them around for my niece and nephew."

"Do you babysit often?" she asked. He certainly seemed to know more about watching children than most bachelors.

He shook his head. "I don't get to watch them all that much because of the rotation. But once in a while one of my brothers and sisters-in-law will ask me to keep one of them when they want to go catch a movie or have a kid-free dinner."

She frowned. "The rotation?"

"I have five brothers," he said, shrugging. "Three of them are married and unless they all want to go out together, my other two brothers and I have to take turns with Mariah."

"Is she your sister?" Heather asked, wondering what it would be like to have that many siblings.

He shook his head. "She's our sister-in-law's sister."

"What happens when the couples go out together?" she asked.

He grinned. "That's when we bachelors get together and become a babysitting tag team."

"That sounds…effective." Laughing, Heather shook her head. "I still can't get over six boys. Your poor parents. I can only imagine the chaos."

"Actually, they're my foster brothers," he said, smiling. "We met as teenagers and finished growing up together on the Last Chance Ranch."

"Oh, I'm sorry," she said, wondering if growing up a foster child was a painful subject for him.

He shook his head. "Don't apologize. Thanks to our foster father, Hank Calvert, moving to his ranch was the best thing that ever happened to all of us. We've become a real family and there's nothing we wouldn't do for each other."

"That's wonderful," she said, meaning it. She had never known that kind of closeness with her sister. If they had been close, Heather wouldn't have had such a struggle the past couple of years.

They were silent for a moment before he asked, "What about you? Do you have brothers and sisters?"

"I have an older sister," she answered, nodding. "But Stephanie and her husband live in Japan and I haven't seen or heard much from her in several years."

"That must be tough," he said, his tone sympathetic.

"I would like to say that it is," she confessed, feeling a twinge of regret. "But my sister and I never really had anything in common, nor were we ever all that close. I always loved growing up on the Circle W and couldn't imagine moving so far away that I wouldn't be able to come back whenever I wanted to ride my horse. But she couldn't wait to grow up and leave it and our family as far behind as her Prada knockoffs could take her." Heather paused as a wave of emotion swept over her. "She didn't even bother to come home for our father's funeral two years ago."

T.J. put his arm around her shoulders and pulled her to his side in a comforting gesture. "It's never too late, Heather. Maybe one day you and your sister can find some common ground."

His companionable hug not only startled her, but when she glanced up to meet his warm hazel gaze, she could tell it had also surprised him. An awkward silence followed the physical connection and neither of them seemed to know what to say. Deciding to put some distance between them, she took a step away from him and started toward her son to take him upstairs.

"I think I should probably go ahead and get Seth settled down for the night," she said, feeling a little breathless.

"I'll help the two of you get upstairs," T.J. said, lifting her baby so that Seth was sitting on T.J.'s forearm.

"Thank you, but I can make it on my own," she said, holding out her arms to take Seth.

But her little boy had other ideas. Shaking his head, he placed his little arm around T.J.'s neck and smiled at her as if to say she didn't have a choice in the matter. He wanted T.J. to carry him and that was that.

As they walked down the hall and up the stairs, Heather couldn't help but wonder if it might not be wise to get a boat for the next time the road flooded. Under normal conditions, it wouldn't be an issue. She, and her parents before her, had always kept plenty of supplies on hand to get them through whenever the creek flooded. But last night she had no choice but to risk being caught on the wrong side of the creek. Seth needed to see a doctor and a trip to the ER had been her only option. But if she had a boat, she would be able to get them home and not have to rely on the generosity of a man who threw her off-guard and caused her son to turn into a deserter.

Of course, getting a boat to cross the floodwaters would be contingent on them still living on the Circle W. And unless a miracle happened, enabling her to pay the back taxes on the ranch, she was going to lose her home and she and her son would have to live elsewhere.

Just the thought of losing the place her family had owned for several generations was more than she could bear, and she decided to wait until she returned home to consider her options. At the moment, the feel of T.J.'s hand at the small of her back, guiding her as they climbed the steps, was distracting and every bit as disconcerting as him giving her a companionable hug.

Heather wasn't the least bit comfortable with what she was feeling. She already had too many things on her plate to worry about an unwanted attraction to her sexy neighbor.

Her heart skipped several beats. She thought T.J. Malloy was sexy? Dear lord, she needed to get home and regain her perspective.

When they reached the room she and her son were sharing, Heather reached to take Seth from T.J. "Thank you again for all you've done for us."

"I'm just doing what any good neighbor would do," he said, shrugging.

T.J. placed Seth in her arms and as T.J.'s eyes locked with hers, she felt as if she could easily become lost in the compassion she detected in his hazel gaze. But as they continued to stare at each other, the air seemed to fill with a charged tension that she hadn't felt in a very long time—not since her fiancé had been killed in an industrial accident shortly after they discovered she was pregnant with Seth.

As the moment stretched into an awkward silence, she cleared her throat and reached for the doorknob. "I'll, um, see you in the morning."

He continued to stare at her for several seconds before he nodded and reached up to trace his finger down her jawline. "Sleep well, Heather."

His deep baritone saying her name and the feel of his feather-light touch caused her heart to flutter wildly and it took everything she had to stop herself from leaning closer. "G-good night, T.J."

Before she made a complete fool of herself, Heather quickly carried her son into the bedroom and closed the door behind them. Had she lost her mind? She still wasn't entirely certain she could trust the man. Why was she feeling flustered and breathless from staring into his mesmerizing hazel eyes? And why hadn't she protested when he touched her?

She wasn't looking for a man to add one more complication to her already difficult life. She had a child to raise and a ranch to try to hold on to. The last thing she needed was any kind of distraction. And that included a seemingly well-meaning cowboy with a hypnotic gaze and the unsettling ability to remind her she was a woman who hadn't been held by a man in quite some time.

Three

The following afternoon, T.J. stood in his driveway and watched Heather's gray sedan drive down the lane toward the main road. Stuffing his hands in the front pockets of his jeans, he sighed heavily. She was almost completely recovered from having the flu and at this point, he was pretty sure there wasn't any danger of her becoming ill again. So why wasn't he all that happy to see her leave?

He still wasn't sure he even liked her. She seemed to take offense to just about everything he said and trying to get her to accept his help when she clearly needed it was like trying to convince birds not to roost in the trees at night. And although they had established a truce of sorts, it was an uneasy one at best.

After last night, when he hugged her in the family

room, then touched her cheek as they said good-night at her bedroom door, things had turned awkward between them. This morning they had both seemed grateful to have Seth to focus on over breakfast and in the hours before she left to go home. Heather read a book to him that she'd had in the diaper bag and T.J. had gotten down on his hands and knees to give the little guy rides around the man cave. So why did he feel let down that she and her kid were leaving?

But as T.J. stood there gazing at the taillights of her car, he had to be honest with himself. He suspected he knew the reason behind her haste to leave the Dusty Diamond and his reluctance to see her go.

And it had nothing whatsoever to do with her wanting to check on her horses or his concern about her having a setback.

Last night he had seen the same awareness in her expressive blue eyes that he was sure she had seen in his. The slight sway of her body when he touched her cheek told him that she'd felt the magnetic pull between them as strongly as he had.

When he watched her car reach the end of the lane and turn onto the main road, he shook his head at his own foolishness and headed toward the barn. Just because Heather Wilson revved his engine didn't mean a damned thing. She was an extremely attractive, single woman who had been staying with him in close quarters and he was a man who had been neglecting his libido for longer than he cared to admit. Naturally he was going to notice how long her legs were and wonder about how they would feel wrapped around him as he sank himself deep inside of her.

T.J. cussed a blue streak when he felt his body start to tighten. Had he lost his mind? Heather Wilson was the last woman he should be getting all hot and bothered about. She wanted to argue with him over everything and just trying to use good manners around her proved to be a powerful struggle. Hell, he didn't really know the woman beyond the fact that she lived on the ranch next to his, she had a horse that was an escape artist and her little boy was cute as a button.

"Hey, boss? You got a minute?"

When T.J. looked up, one of his men was walking toward him from the far end of the barn.

"Sure," he answered, thankful that the sandy-haired cowboy had interrupted his train of thought. "What's on your mind, Tommy Lee?"

"Didn't you tell me Ms. Wilson's men had the weekend off?" the man asked as he strolled up to him.

T.J. nodded. "They should be back on Monday. Why?"

"I don't know if this means anything," the man said. "But earlier, when I was over at the Wilson place feeding the horses, I noticed something that didn't seem quite right."

"What's that?" T.J. queried, frowning. "When I sent Harry over there yesterday, he didn't mention seeing anything out of the ordinary. What did you see that he didn't?"

"I probably wouldn't have noticed myself, but last night when it stormed the wind blew kind of hard and must have blown Ms. Wilson's bunkhouse door open. When I went to pull it shut, I got a look inside." Tommy Lee shook his head. "There weren't any signs of it being lived in and it didn't look like it had been used in quite a while. Everything was real dusty and it had that stale smell like when a place is closed up for a long time."

T.J. frowned. Heather's men might live elsewhere, but that was unlikely. The area was comprised of large ranches and since a working cowboy's day started well before dawn, it was a matter of convenience for the men to live on the outfit where they worked, or at least nearby. Even T.J.'s foreman, Dan, and his family lived in one of the two small houses T.J. had built on the property when he bought the Dusty Diamond, in anticipation of some of the men he hired being married.

"Anyway, I just thought I'd let you know," Tommy Lee continued, shrugging.

"Thanks for passing along the information," T.J. answered. "I appreciate it, Tommy Lee."

"Do you want me to go over there again tomorrow mornin' to do the feedin'?" the man asked as he started back toward the end of the barn where he had been repairing a stall door.

"No, I'll go over there first thing in the morning to take care of her horses and check things out for myself," T.J. said as he entered the tack room.

He knew he should probably let one of his men take care of going over to Heather's tomorrow. It was really none of his business about her men and he was certain she would tell him as much. But he wanted to check

on her and Seth anyway and he refused to delve too
deeply into the reasons why.

Taking one of the lead ropes hanging on a hook
on the wall, he couldn't stop thinking about what he
had just learned. As he walked to one of the stalls to
get the sorrel gelding he'd been training he wondered
why Heather had let on like she had given her men the
weekend off if she didn't have anyone working for her.
Did that mean she was trying to run the Circle W by
herself? With a kid and a case of the flu?

He led the horse back to the tack room to saddle
him. T.J. wasn't sure what the deal was with Heather
Wilson. But he had every intention of finding out.

If, as he suspected, she was trying to run her ranch
on her own—without *any* help—it would explain a lot.

Whenever her stallion had gotten onto his property,
he'd wondered why she hadn't immediately instructed
her men to make the needed repairs to the fence to
keep it from happening again. It was not only the mark
of a good rancher to keep his fences in decent condi-
tion, but it was also the neighborly thing to do to keep
your animals from being a nuisance. But if there was
no one working for her, there wasn't any way Heather
could have mended her fences with a baby in her arms.

The guilt he had experienced after she explained
that she had tried to keep the stallion confined in-
creased tenfold. She had either been too stubborn or
too proud to explain things and ask for his help. From
being around her the past couple of days, he suspected
it was a combination of both.

Shaking his head at her obstinacy, he finished saddling the gelding. Just as he secured the cinch his cell phone rang. "What's up, Nate?" he asked when he recognized his brother's number on the caller ID.

"When we got to talking about my new place the other night, I forgot to ask what you want me to bring to the New Year's Eve party." Nate paused a moment before adding, "And keep in mind that I don't know beans from buckshot about cooking so it will have to be something I can buy that's already prepared."

"Don't worry about it," T.J. answered. "Taylor volunteered herself and Bria to handle the food." Taylor had been a personal chef before she married Lane and the woman was as passionate about food as she was about their brother—and Bria was the best home cook in central Texas.

"You know we really lucked out in the sisters-in-law department," Nate commented. "Bria and Taylor are the best cooks in the whole damned state and Summer loves to plan all the other details for our get-togethers. We don't have to do a thing but show up."

T.J. chuckled. "Like you'd do anything even if they didn't."

"Hey, like I told you. I could buy food that's already cooked to bring to the parties," Nate answered, sounding quite pleased with himself about that contribution.

"What are you going to do when you move to Twin Oaks Ranch?" T.J. asked, laughing. "You'll eventually get tired of slapping a piece of meat between two slices of bread or zapping something in the microwave."

"I'll do the same as you, smart-ass," Nate retorted. "I'll hire a housekeeper who cooks."

"Touché, Romeo." T.J. laughed out loud. "I didn't think you'd made any plans past fixing up your ranch house into a pleasure palace." He couldn't help but grin. "Maybe you're finally starting to grow up."

"Nah." Nate laughed. "Then I'd be too much like your sorry hide."

"What's wrong with that?" T.J. asked, going along with his brother's good-natured ribbing.

"If I was like you, I'd strike out every time I tried to talk to a woman." Nate grunted. "You know as much about women as I know about cooking."

"Oh, really?" T.J. knew better, but asked anyway. "What makes you say that?"

"Take your neighbor lady for example. Instead of showing her your ornery side when you took her horse back to her, you should have turned on the charm," Nate said as if he was an expert on the subject of the fairer sex. "You should have smiled and had a friendly little chat with her about something like the weather or that new steakhouse up in Stephenville—anything other than the real reason you were there. By the time you got around to leaving, I'm betting she'd have offered to have her hired hands fix that fence without you even having to bring up the subject. You would have gotten what you wanted and she'd have thought it was her idea to take care of it for you."

T.J.'s good humor suddenly drained away like water running through a sieve. Heather and his run-ins with her had been a touchy subject with him before, but after getting to know her a little better over the past couple of days and learning that she might be trying to run the

Circle W without any kind of help, he felt too guilty to discuss the matter with anyone, and especially not with his skirt-chasing brother.

Of course, Nate had no way of knowing any of the details about the past forty-eight hours and T.J. had no intention of enlightening him. But Nate's comments were hitting a little too close to what T.J. had already figured out for himself—he'd been a prized jackass in his handling of the situation.

Deciding it was definitely time for a change in the direction of their conversation, he knew exactly what to say to distract Nate. "So how's that kind of thinking working out for you with that little blonde over in Waco?" T.J. asked.

She was the only woman Nate had ever returned to after moving on to other conquests, and their on-again, off-again relationship had the entire family speculating if she was the one who would finally cure Nate of his wild ways.

There was a long pause and T.J. wasn't sure his brother hadn't hung up on him.

"Jessica and I aren't seeing each other anymore," Nate finally said, sounding a little less sure of himself.

"Again? Want to talk about it?" T.J. asked.

"There's nothing much to say," Nate said, his tone quiet. "She wants one thing and I want another."

They were both silent for several long moments before T.J. offered, "You know any one of us will listen if you change your mind."

"Hey, you know me. I'm just fine." Nate's laughter sounded a bit forced. "I like keeping my options open."

They talked a few more minutes before ending the call, then T.J. clipped his cell phone to his belt and led the sorrel gelding from the barn into the adjoining indoor arena. Mounting the horse, he used the reins to guide it into the series of moves that would be expected of the animal and its rider during competition. But as the horse executed the patterns flawlessly, T.J.'s mind was on other things.

Nate clearly wasn't as good with women as he let on, not if the blonde was breaking things off between them. Unfortunately, there wasn't anything T.J. could do about his brother's situation. But there was, however, something he could do about the situation with Heather and her son.

First thing tomorrow morning, he fully intended to go over to the Circle W and assess the situation for himself. If it turned out that she was indeed on her own over there, as he strongly suspected, she could talk until she was blue in the face but he wasn't going to take no for an answer.

He was going to help Heather. And in the bargain, assuage his conscience for being such a jerk about her horse.

Heather yawned and finished putting Seth's coat and hat on him, then lifted him into the strap-on baby carrier she was wearing.

"As soon as we feed the horses and muck out the stalls, you can take a nap while I see if I can find a few extra dollars in the budget to fix the roof over the utility room."

In answer, her son smiled at her and sleepily laid his head against her breast. While she fed the horses and mucked out stalls, Seth would doze on and off and babble to her about the horses, which he loved. Then he'd sleep for another half hour or so after they returned to the house. It wasn't easy working with a toddler strapped to her chest and the chores took almost twice the amount of time that they would have taken otherwise, but after almost a year and a half of having to do it this way, she and Seth were both used to the routine.

As she left the house, Heather noticed a pickup truck with the Dusty Diamond logo painted on the side parked beside her ancient Toyota. Why wasn't she surprised that T.J. had again sent one of his men over to take care of the chores? She'd never met a man more determined to have his way. He had decided that she didn't need to be out doing the chores and he was doing everything he could to make sure she wasn't.

But when she started across the yard, she looked up to find that it was T.J. himself standing in the barn's wide doorway. Her heart skipped a beat. As much as she would like to ignore her reaction, just the sight of the man caused her to catch her breath. Leaning one shoulder against the door, he had his arms folded across his broad chest and his long blue-jean-clad legs crossed casually at the ankles. But his wide-brimmed, black hat was pulled down low on his forehead and he wore the same dark scowl that she had seen each time he'd brought her stallion back.

A twinge of disappointment ran through her. Just

when she had started to think he really was one of the good guys, he had apparently returned to being the disapproving, judgmental neighbor.

"What are you doing here, Malloy?" she asked, aggravated with herself for giving his rugged good looks and the return of his ornery disposition a second thought.

"I came to take care of your horses and check to see if you and Seth are all right," he said, his tone flat.

"As you can see we're both doing fine and I'm perfectly capable of taking care of my own horses," she answered, stopping in front of him. "Now if you'll excuse me, I need to get that done."

Uncrossing his big booted feet, he straightened, blocking her entry into the barn. "I've already fed them and after I turned them out into the pasture for some exercise, I mucked out the stalls and put down fresh straw. They're already back in their stalls and should be good until tomorrow."

"How long have you been here?" she asked, disturbed by the fact that he had been on the property for at least a couple of hours without her realizing he was even there.

What if he'd been someone else? Someone who was up to no good? A thief would have been able to take anything he wanted and she would have been none the wiser. Or worse yet, someone could have broken into the house before she'd had the chance to retrieve her father's old shotgun that hung above the fireplace mantel in the living room.

Not that retrieving the shotgun would have done

a lot of good. It had a broken trigger and hadn't been capable of firing in more than twenty years. Not to mention the fact that she wasn't even sure how to load it. But just the sight of the gun might be enough to intimidate someone into leaving her and her son alone.

"I got here around dawn and it was long enough to know that you haven't been completely honest with me, Heather." He nodded toward the house. "It's still pretty damp and chilly. Why don't we go inside? We can talk there."

"There's nothing to discuss," Heather said, standing her ground. "I haven't been dishonest with you."

At least, technically she hadn't been. She'd just omitted a few facts.

His frown darkened and a muscle twitched along his lean jaw when it started to rain. "*Please* could we go inside the house to talk before we all get drenched? That wouldn't be good for you or Seth."

"I really need to take inventory of my supplies," she hedged. "I'll be going into town to the feed store tomorrow and I want to make sure I get everything."

She could tell from his determined expression that T.J. wasn't going to give up.

"You need oats, hay and straw," he said, placing his arm around her shoulders to turn her and Seth back toward the house. "But I think you already knew that."

Heather didn't protest further as they crossed the yard and entered the house. For one thing, she needed to get her son out of the weather. And for another, she was too distracted by the comforting feel of T.J.'s arm holding her close to his side.

She knew he was only trying to shield her and Seth from the rain, but that did little to lessen the effect his nearness was having on her. His clean masculine scent, combined with the rich smell of leather and the heat from his body, seemed to warm her all the way to her soul.

"Let me hold him while you take off your coat," T.J. said as they entered the house. Shrugging out of his leather jacket, he draped it over one of the kitchen chairs as she unfastened the sides of the toddler carrier. He smiled as he turned to lift her son. "Hey there, little guy. Did you miss me?"

Seth jabbered a sleepy greeting before laying his head on T.J.'s shoulder.

While she hung her jacket in the laundry room to dry, T.J. took off Seth's hat and coat. When she returned to the kitchen her chest tightened at the sight of T.J. swaying back and forth with her son snuggled against his broad chest. How many times over the past two years had she regretted that Seth and her late fiancé had been cheated out of a father-and-son relationship?

Heather frowned. She would have expected to resent any man except her fiancé having that special time with her son. But she didn't. She found it endearing and that bothered her.

Of all the men to be tender and caring with her son, she would have never expected it from T. J. Malloy, nor was she sure she was comfortable with it. She didn't want to see Seth start to care for T.J. and then be disappointed or hurt when the man lost interest in them.

"He's asleep," T.J. said quietly. "Where do you want me to lay him down?"

She showed T.J. down the hall to Seth's small bedroom. He got Seth settled in his bed and she and T.J. walked back into the kitchen before Heather spoke. "I assume by now you've figured out that I'm operating the Circle W on a shoestring," she said, resigned to the fact that T.J. wasn't going to leave without an explanation.

Nodding, he pulled out a chair at the round oak table, sat down and causally rested the ankle of one leg on the knee of the other as if he didn't have a care in the world. "How long have you been trying to run things without help?"

She sighed. At this point, there was no sense in being evasive. He'd been in the barn and she was certain he'd observed how many repairs needed to be made, as well as how little she kept on hand in the way of supplies. He probably even knew that the bunk house hadn't seen a hired hand in more than a year.

"After my father died, I managed to keep the two men who worked for him until Seth was about four months old."

"So the better part of two years," he said, frowning.

"Yes."

"Why didn't you tell me you were alone over here with a baby whenever I brought your horse back?" he demanded.

"The first time you had to bring Magic back, I wasn't even home," she answered defensively. "You put him in the corral and left a note fastened to the gate, asking me to keep him off your land."

"You could have told me one of the other times when you were at home," he said pointedly. "I would have been more understanding if you had. I could have helped you."

"Oh, give me a break, Malloy." She shook her head. "You were too angry to listen even if I had tried to explain." Suddenly irritated by his tone and the accusatory expression on his handsome face, she added, "Besides, it wasn't any of your business then and to tell you the truth, it's none of your concern now."

"I would have helped you out," he repeated, apparently choosing to ignore the warning in her voice. "I could have at least had my men take care of repairing your fences for you."

"I'm not a charity case." Her anger grew with each passing second when she detected the sympathy in his hazel gaze. She didn't want anyone feeling sorry for her or thinking that she was incapable of doing things herself. And especially not T. J. Malloy. She wasn't sure why, but she couldn't stand him thinking that she was a helpless wimp. "And I certainly don't need or want your pity."

"I never said you were a charity case," he said gently as he rose to his feet. The tone of his voice caused an unfamiliar softening deep inside of her. "But there's nothing wrong with neighbors helping each other out. It doesn't mean that I feel sorry for you. I'm just trying to do what I feel is right."

"You've performed your neighborly duty for the

past few days," she said, her heart skipping a beat as he approached. "And I really appreciate your assistance, but…"

Her voice trailed off as he stopped within inches of her. Tipping up her chin with his index finger, he lifted her head until their gazes met. "Heather, I'm really sorry for being a jerk about your horse. But honestly, I'm not an unreasonable man. I swear I would have listened and understood if you'd only explained the situation."

His deep voice had a soothing effect on her and when he put his arms loosely around her waist and leaned forward, she couldn't have stopped him if her life depended on it. Brushing her lips with his, the kiss was soft and brief, and wasn't meant to excite. Unfortunately, she found the caress to be one of the sexiest she could ever remember and she responded by swaying closer to him.

As his mouth settled over hers, his arms tightened around her. Heather tried to remind herself why allowing T.J. to kiss her wasn't a good idea. But as he traced her lips with his tongue, her eyes drifted shut and she couldn't think of one single reason to call a halt to the caress.

Without a thought to what she was doing, she raised her arms to his shoulders and tangled her fingers in the soft brown curls at the nape of his neck. Her heart sped up when he coaxed her mouth to open for him. Slipping his tongue inside, he deepened the kiss. As he explored her with tender care, a warmth she hadn't felt in a very long time began to flow through every part of her. Her knees felt as if they would give way as he lightly stroked her inner recesses.

The sudden sound of thunder rumbling, followed closely by rain pounding on the roof in what could only be described as another Texas gully washer, helped to clear the haze from her obviously foggy brain. She pushed away from him as her senses returned.

"I'm sorry," he said, releasing her immediately. "I was out of line."

"No. I mean, yes." She shook her head as she tried to gather her thoughts. She hurried into the laundry room to escape. "There's something I have to do."

Finding the buckets she used when it rained, she placed one under the drip coming from the ceiling between the clothes dryer and the water heater. When she turned around, T.J. was standing in the doorway, watching her.

"A leaky roof was one of the reasons you were so anxious to leave the Dusty Diamond, wasn't it?" he asked. "You needed to make sure the buckets didn't overflow."

She nodded as she placed another one of the pails next to the furnace. "I haven't had time to make the repairs."

"When did it start leaking?" he asked, his gaze holding hers as she straightened and turned to face him.

"This past summer." She shrugged. "One of the really severe storms blew off several shingles and I haven't had the opportunity to replace them."

"That was in the spring," he said, folding his arms across his broad chest.

His stance and the tone of his voice were unmistakably disapproving and it not only erased any lingering traces of warmth she felt from his kiss, but it also reignited her anger. It was easy for him to pass judgment. He wasn't the one struggling to make ends meet while trying to raise a child alone and find the extra funds needed for the innumerable things around the Circle W in need of repair or replacement. Nor was he the one who would seem vulnerable if he reached out for help.

"Thank you for stopping by to take care of my horses, but you won't have to bother with helping me again," she said, brushing past him as she walked into the kitchen to retrieve his jacket. She handed it to him and moved to the back door. "I'm sure you have more important things to do with your time than to take me to task over things that are absolutely none of your business."

T.J. stared at her for a moment as if he wanted to argue the point. Then he pulled on his coat. "If you need help with anything don't hesitate to give me a call."

"I'll keep that in mind," she said as she opened the door. "But don't worry about us. Seth and I will be just fine."

T.J. had no sooner cleared the entrance than the door was forcefully shut behind him. Hearing the distinct sound of the dead bolt being set, he shook his head.

"So much for being a good neighbor," he muttered as he pulled his hat down low to shield his face from the rain and jogged the short distance to his truck.

She was pissed off again and unless he missed his guess, it was more a matter of her stinging pride than anything he had said. It was crystal clear she needed help—both with the work around the ranch and repairs to the house. But if there was one thing he had learned in the past several days, Heather Wilson was way too proud for her own good.

Why did she feel the need to prove herself? Why was she scared to death that someone would see her situation and look down on her for having such a struggle?

And he had no doubt that she was having a tough time of things. Although the horses were well taken care of, the amount of supplies she had told him better than anything else that she was hurting financially. Most ranchers tried to keep enough feed and bedding on hand to last for a couple of weeks, at the very least. Heather barely had enough for the next couple of days. And if her flimsy excuse about needing to take inventory of her supplies hadn't been enough to convince him of how embarrassed she was by her circumstances, the heightened color on her cheeks as she tried to explain about her leaking roof was.

Cursing the woman's stubborn pride, he started the truck and drove down the lane to the main road, turning toward the Dusty Diamond. If she would let him, he could make things a hell of a lot easier for her. But he had a feeling they would be passing out ice water in hell before that happened.

As he stared out the windshield he had to concentrate hard on the road ahead. The wipers were on the fastest setting, but couldn't keep up with the amount of rain falling. He suddenly brought the truck to a stop and uttered a string of cuss words that would have raised a sailor's eyebrows. He had been so distracted by Heather and what he'd observed of her ranch that he had forgotten all about the swollen creek and the inevitable flooding. Fortunately, the water always receded quickly once it stopped raining, but it didn't appear that the rain was going to ease up anytime soon.

Staring through the sheets of water running down the windshield, T.J. decided he only had two options. He could either sit in his truck in the middle of the road for what could turn out to be the rest of the day and night or he could turn it around and go back to the Circle W.

Given the choices, there was really only one thing he could do. Heather wasn't going to be overly happy about it—and for that matter neither was he—but there wasn't any way around it. He was going to have to stay at her place until the road cleared.

A few minutes later, he parked the truck in front of her house, got out and jogged across the yard. He took the back porch steps two at a time. Drawing in a deep breath, he raised his arm to knock.

"The road is flooded out," he said when Heather opened the door.

She stared past him at the heavy rain just beyond the porch, then, sighing audibly, she stepped back for him to enter the house.

"I'll set another place for lunch," she said, sounding resigned. "You're going to be here a while."

Four

After an uncomfortably silent lunch with her unexpected guest, Heather was glad when T.J. took Seth into the living room to play while she washed the dishes and cleaned up the kitchen. She needed the distance between them to figure out why she seemed to lose all common sense whenever she was around him.

Normally, she was a very even-tempered, rational woman. Maybe she had a little more pride than was good for her and she was pretty stubborn about some things, but she didn't know anyone who didn't have a few flaws. But there was nothing about her behavior when she was near T.J. that made a bit of sense. He seemed to have the ability to anger her beyond words one minute, then turn around and have her melting into his arms without a thought about why she shouldn't, the next.

But as she thought about her irritation with him earlier this morning, she had to admit to herself that part of the problem was her overwhelming embarrassment about her situation. It was humiliating to let anyone see how run-down the Circle W had become in the two and a half years since her father had passed away. Especially a man like T.J., who had family and more money to spare than most people saw in their entire lives. At one time the ranch had been one of the finest in the county, raising registered quarter horses for competition in the pleasure class at horse shows, as well as supplying a couple of dude ranches over in New Mexico with horses for their trail rides. But now? Seeing the Circle W through the eyes of a stranger, she was certain that it just looked shabby and sad.

When her father had been alive and well, he had at least half a dozen hired hands working for him, close to a hundred horses grazing in the pastures and the barns and outbuildings had been painted a striking red with white trim. The board fences and house had always been kept a pristine white, the trees and shrubs were always neatly trimmed and everything was in excellent repair. But in the years following his death, Heather hadn't had the time or the money to keep up with everything. The roof leaked, fences needed mending, paint was peeling and the trees and shrubs were overgrown and shapeless.

Her breath caught on a sob as she thought about the assurance she had given her dying father as he lay sick in the hospital with end-stage cancer. He had begged her to hang on to the ranch that had been in his family for over a hundred and fifty years and she had given him her word that she would. But that promise was quickly becoming one she was finding almost impossible to keep.

That hurt more than anything else. Not being able to honor his last wish was going to be one of the biggest disappointments of her life.

She and her father had always been extremely close. He had been her best friend and taught her everything she knew about ranching. She often thought that closeness had played a part in why there was an emotional distance between her and her sister.

Stephanie was actually her half sister—her mother's daughter from a previous marriage. From what Heather had learned over the years, her father had doted on Stephanie until Heather was born. After that, he didn't seem to have as much time for his stepdaughter and Stephanie clearly resented Heather for that.

"Heather, do you need help?" T.J. asked, from behind her.

"No, I just finished up in here," she said, shaking her head.

She had been so lost in her disturbing thoughts that she hadn't noticed his approach. But she noticed it now. He was so close, she could feel the delightful heat from his body. A shiver of awareness coursed through her and, making sure she kept her back to him, she quickly swiped away the moisture that had gathered in her eyes before she turned to face him.

"Where's Seth?"

"In his bed." T.J. laughed. "I think I wore him out. We played for quite a while with a little barn that mooed every time the door was opened. Then he yawned a couple of times, crawled up in my lap and went to sleep."

"Thank you for watching him while I got things cleared away from lunch," she said as she turned to start the coffeemaker. "It isn't always easy trying to get things done while watching him, too."

T.J. smiled. "Seth's a great little kid. I enjoy spending time with him."

Heather took a deep breath and released the last of her lingering anger. It wasn't T.J.'s fault her ranch was so run-down and it was past time that she stopped taking her frustration out on him.

"It's still raining and it looks like you'll be here awhile." She reached in the cabinet for two mugs. "Would you like some coffee?"

"Sure." He was silent for several long moments before he commented, "We've had more rain in the past couple of days than I can ever remember at this time of year."

"It has been unusual," she agreed, walking over to set a mug of coffee in front of him.

As they stared at each other she was reminded of how comforting it was to have another adult to talk to. She had been so busy taking care of Seth and the ranch, she hadn't had time to think about how truly alone she had been.

The moment stretched into awkwardness and she

knew of only one way to ease the tension. When she lowered herself onto the chair across from him, they stared silently at each other a few seconds longer before she finally took a deep breath. "I'm sorry for the way I reacted earlier today when I discovered you fed the horses and then later when you asked me about the leaking roof."

He eyed her over the rim of the raised coffee cup in his hand before he responded. "I just wanted to help." Shaking his head, he added, "But like you said, what you do on your ranch really isn't any of my business."

"That isn't an excuse for my being hostile toward you," she said, feeling worse about her behavior by the minute. He had done nothing but try to help her and she'd been nothing but ungrateful. Of course, she had been sick and thoroughly worn-out. But she suspected it had more to do with not being used to confiding in anyone for longer than she cared to remember.

Sighing, she admitted, "I was…embarrassed."

Setting his mug on the table, he nodded. "I thought that might be the case. But I swear, I wasn't being judgmental when I asked how long the roof had been leaking."

"The Circle W hasn't always looked like this or been in this bad of shape," she said, staring at the hot, black liquid in the cup in front of her. "It used to be the nicest horse ranch in the county." She took a deep breath to chase away the sense of regret that always came over her when she thought about how things used to be, and what she'd lost. "It's just been hard for me to keep up with everything the past couple of years."

"Since you had Seth?" he mused.

"The money problems actually started a few months before that when my father passed away," she admitted. She wasn't certain why it was important to her that T.J. understand her circumstances. It just was. "Insurance took care of most of Dad's treatment, but it didn't cover everything." Holding her coffee mug with both hands in an attempt to stop them from trembling, she added, "After I used what money my dad had in savings to pay off the medical bills, I managed to keep the only two men left who worked for him until after I had Seth. Once he was old enough to stay in a baby carrier, so I could take him with me to do the chores, I had to let the men go."

Raising her gaze to meet his, her chest tightened at the compassion she saw in his eyes.

"That's when your stallion started getting out to come over to my place?" he asked.

She nodded. "Between trying to take care of a baby and run the whole ranch by myself, I didn't have the time to repair the fences and there was no one to help me do it."

"So you've been here by yourself for a year and a half?" T.J. frowned. "What about Seth's daddy? Couldn't he have helped you?"

"Seth's father was killed in an industrial accident shortly after we found out I was pregnant," she said, shaking her head.

"I'm sorry, Heather."

Her chest tightened with emotion at the sincerity

in his voice. It felt good to finally be able to talk to someone about it.

"Thank you, T.J." She swallowed around the lump clogging her throat. "I won't pretend that it wasn't one of the toughest times of my life—losing my fiancé and my father within a few months of each other—but I got through it. I have a beautiful son and although we don't have much of a family left, we have each other."

They were silent for a few moments before he spoke again. "I know it's none of my business, but how have you been making ends meet?"

She paused for a moment. The concern she detected and the gentle tone of his voice made her feel that he actually did care. The feeling was unexpected and coupled with how attractive she found him, it could prove to be a disastrous combination for her.

Maybe telling him a little more about her situation would help to cool some of those feelings. She shrugged. "I get a small check each month from an annuity my fiancé set up shortly before he was killed and although I don't like it, when I have to, I sell one of the brood mares."

He looked taken aback. "I didn't realize—"

"You're not the only one with a breeding program," she interrupted, smiling. "Magic Dancer is an American Quarter Horse Association world-champion pleasure horse and before my dad retired him from competition, that stallion won in several different age classes." She rose to refill their coffee cups. "Quite a few of his colts have won world championships in their classes and even my brood mares come from champion bloodlines."

"In other words, your stallion didn't spoil my mares, he may have improved my program." T.J. frowned as he sat forward. "I knew his confirmation was outstanding, but I didn't realize he was a registered quarter horse. Why didn't you tell me that instead of letting me rant about keeping him on your property and how he had spoiled my mares?"

Heather laughed as she set his refilled cup on the table. "If you had stopped to take a breath when you were reading me the riot act, I might have."

When she started to return to the opposite side of the table T.J. caught her hand in his. "Why don't we start over and forget about what's happened before I found you and Seth stranded on my side of the creek?" he asked as he pulled her down to sit on his lap.

Instead of her confessions pushing him away, he seemed even more eager to explore this attraction between them.

Unsure of what he was up to, Heather merely nodded as she stared into his incredible hazel eyes. A deep forest green with a halo of brown around the pupils, they seemed to have a hypnotic effect on her. She couldn't work up so much as a hint of a protest.

"Wh-why not make the fresh start now instead of three days ago?" she asked when she finally found her voice.

His slow smile sent her pulse racing and caused a flutter deep in the pit of her stomach. "If we did that, I would be obligated to forget how cute you looked wearing my flannel shirt and how long and shapely your legs are." With one arm around her waist, he held her securely against him as he reached up to cup her cheek with his other hand. "That's something that I just can't do." His eyes darkened. "And as long as we're clearing the air, I have my own confession to make."

Her heart skipped a beat. "What would that be, T.J.?"

"I may have been out of line when I kissed you, but I don't regret it one damned bit," he said, his tone low and intimate. "In fact, I'd really like to kiss you again."

"That probably wouldn't be…a good idea," she said, finding it hard to draw in enough air.

"Why not, Heather?" he asked as he slowly stroked her cheek with the pad of his thumb.

She was sure there were some very good reasons why kissing him again would be unwise. At the moment she couldn't think of a single one. His touch was making her feel warm all over, and her ability to think rationally was all but impossible.

"Did you like when I kissed you earlier?" he persisted.

Heaven help her, but she couldn't have lied to him if she had tried. "Yes. I liked it very much."

"Then why don't I go ahead and kiss you now?" he asked, his smile so darned sexy she was certain he could charm the birds right out of the trees. "We can discuss why it wasn't a good idea later."

Before she had a chance to respond, his firm lips settled over hers. Closing her eyes, Heather gave up trying to remember why she should call a halt to the caress. As he traced the seam of her mouth with his tongue, it suddenly didn't matter anymore. The mingled scents of expensive leather and warm, virile male surrounded her and she opened for him, her body asking him to deepen the kiss, and she didn't give her submission a second thought.

Exploring her with soft gentle strokes of his tongue, he sent heat flowing through her body as he slid his hand from her cheek down to her collarbone. But when he continued down the slope of her breast to cup her fullness with his large palm, he created a longing deep within her that she had almost forgotten existed. She knew without a doubt that she could easily lose herself in the feelings T.J. was creating.

The hardness of his building arousal against her hip should have been enough warning to bring her to her senses, but his desire only heightened the need swirling deep inside of her. As more ribbons of heat threaded their way throughout her entire body, Heather remembered that it had been over two and a half years since she'd experienced even the slightest stirrings of passion. She had been so busy being a caregiver, a single mother and the owner and manager of a ranch in deep financial crisis that she had forgotten what it felt like to be a woman in the arms of a man who desired her.

A tiny moan escaped her when T.J. slowly slid his hand down her side to her hip, then to her knee and back up along the inside of her thigh. Even through her jeans his touch caused her to tingle all over. Unable to sit still, she moved her own hands to unfasten the first few snaps on his chambray shirt. When she rested her palms on his bare chest, the feel of his hard muscles and the steady beating of his heart caused a yearning inside of her that robbed her of breath.

As he eased away from the kiss, T.J. nibbled his way along her jaw to whisper in her ear, "I think I'm going to go out to the barn for a little while, sweetheart."

His warm breath sent goose bumps shimmering over her skin, and Heather blinked as her hazy brain tried to grasp what he had said. "B-but you've already taken care of the horses. There really isn't anything left to do out there until tomorrow."

His low chuckle caused a delicious shiver to slide up her spine as he set her on her feet then rose from the chair only to pull her back into his arms.

"Yes, but if I don't go somewhere to cool off for a while, one of two things is going to happen right now. We'll either end up doing something you're not ready for or I'll end up losing my sanity." He kissed the tip of her nose. "I'll be back in time to babysit Seth while you make supper."

As she watched T.J. step back to fasten the snaps on his shirt, then shrug into his jacket and leave the house, Heather swallowed hard. Although need still ran through her veins, she had to thank the stars above that he'd had the presence of mind to end the kiss.

What had she been thinking? Getting involved with T. J. Malloy—or any other man—at this point in her life would be insane. She had a ranch she was trying to hold on to. She had her son's welfare to think about and the last thing she needed was to add to her stress by entering into any kind of emotional or physical involvement.

Of course, she could be overreacting to the situation. Just because there was an undeniable chemistry drawing them together didn't mean anything. All most men needed to become aroused was a warm, willing woman.

Her cheeks heated as she thought about her reaction to him. She certainly hadn't shown even the slightest bit of reluctance. He probably thought she was an easy conquest. Or worse yet, desperate for the attention of a man.

Shaking her head at her behavior, she put their coffee cups in the sink and walked down the hall to check on her son. T.J. was most likely only looking for a good time, and although she hadn't exactly shown him differently, she wasn't a no-strings kind of woman. She had a little boy who was counting on her to protect him—from homelessness *and* from men with no intention of getting serious about a family—and that was exactly what she intended to do.

As she looked in on Seth, she made a silent vow to be stronger and wiser than she'd been before. She wasn't going to allow T.J. to get too close and risk her son becoming too attached to him only to have T.J. move on when he'd had his fill of her. Her suffering the disappointment of being rejected by a man was one thing, but she'd walk through fire before she allowed it to happen to her son.

* * *

"Do 'gain," Seth said, laughing.

"Again?" T.J. let loose with an exaggerated groan. "Wouldn't you rather play with the barn that moos when you open the door?"

"No," the toddler said, giggling happily. "Wide hossy."

He knew that when he gave Seth another ride around the living room perched atop his back, the little boy would want more. But the kid seemed to enjoy listening to T.J. groan about it and Seth thought it was extremely funny when T.J. gave in. Knowing the toddler was having fun was all it took to keep T.J. on his hands and knees and crawling around on the floor.

"The two of you seem to be getting along pretty well in here," Heather commented as she walked into the living room from the kitchen.

"Hossy," Seth said, patting T.J. on the back of the head.

Nodding, she looked from T.J. to Seth. "He's a great horsey, but it's time for you to have a bath, little man, and get ready for bed."

"No," Seth insisted. "Wide hossy."

"Seth." There was a warning in Heather's voice that T.J. new wouldn't be wise for either him or Seth to ignore.

"Would it be all right for me to give him one last ride?" T.J. asked, mindful that it was Heather's call. He didn't want to disappoint the kid, but he didn't want to piss off the boy's mother by interfering with her parenting, either.

"Pease?" Seth begged from T.J.'s back.

"Please?" T.J. echoed, grinning.

"Ganging up on me is not fair," she warned. "But all right. One more ride then it's time for your bath and bed, Seth."

"Otay," Seth said happily as he tugged on the back of T.J.'s shirt. "Go hossy."

Groaning, T.J. got the giggle out of Seth he was looking for and made another trip around the living room, stopping in front of Heather.

"Okay, partner," T.J. said, straightening when she lifted the little boy from his back. "Time for you to take a bath and me to chill out for a little while in front of the TV."

"I'll be back in few minutes," she said, carrying Seth down the hall.

While Heather gave her son a bath and got him ready for bed, T.J. sat down on the couch and used the remote to turn on the television. He really wasn't interested in watching a show, but when Heather returned a distraction might help ease the awkwardness that had developed between them since he'd left the house to go out to the barn earlier that afternoon.

When he'd fed her horses that morning, he had noticed several stalls in need of repair. So, this afternoon, when he'd had enough adrenaline flowing through his veins to bench-press a dump truck, he'd hammered nails into every loose board he could find. By the time he returned to the house an hour or so later, Heather hadn't had a lot to say to him and he was pretty sure he knew why.

He was willing to bet everything he had that while he'd been trying to expend his pent-up energy, she had been thinking about the chemistry between them and how fast it had threatened to flare out of control. He'd seen the heat in her eyes after that kiss and, knowing the way women had of stewing on things, she had probably talked herself out of letting it happen again.

He frowned. He'd realized there was a mutual attraction between them when she'd first stepped out of her car the night she and Seth stayed at his place. Hell, he would have to be nine kinds of a fool not to have noticed the spark. But he hadn't anticipated the pull to be so intense and he knew beyond a shadow of doubt that Heather hadn't, either. Their chemistry had scared her and, to tell the truth, he wasn't overly comfortable with it himself. He liked his life the way it was. He wasn't looking for anything long-term. He came and went as he pleased and didn't have anyone he had to answer to. But he wasn't sure it was going to be possible to ignore whatever this was that was happening with them.

When he'd pulled her down onto his lap after their conversation over coffee, he had only meant to offer his compassion for all she'd been through. Losing both her fiancé and her father within such a short time, then facing single motherhood without any kind of support system, had to have been extremely hard for her. That kind of heartbreak on top of heartbreak would have destroyed a lot of women. And on top of that, she'd been running the whole Circle W outfit by herself. He honestly didn't know how she'd managed.

Heather was a survivor and he wanted her to know how much he admired her. But the minute he had her in his arms, his good sense seemed to desert him completely. All he had ended up doing was showing her that he had about as much control over his hormones as a teenaged boy on prom night.

Disgusted with himself and too restless to sit still, T.J. shook his head and got up to look out the window. It had stopped raining, but it would be some time tomorrow before the road cleared. At least he would be able to tend to her horses in the morning before he had to go back to his ranch.

As he stood there wondering what else he could do to help Heather, Seth ran up beside him, grinning. The little boy patted T.J.'s thigh to get his full attention. Jabbering something T.J. couldn't understand, Seth reached up and took T.J. by the hand to tug him along.

"Seth," Heather said firmly, hurrying into the room. There was no denying the irritation in her tone. "It's time for bed."

Reaching down, T.J. picked up the toddler then turned to face Heather. "Was he telling me goodnight?"

She hesitated a moment before she shook her head. "No, he wants you to tuck him into bed."

"I think that can be arranged," T.J. said, laughing as he ruffled the little boy's copper-colored hair. "I like your pajamas, partner. I wish I had a pair with horses on them."

To his surprise Seth wrapped his arms around T.J.'s

neck and hugged him, then gave him a rather juicy kiss on the cheek. "Go bed now."

Heather didn't look happy as he carried Seth down the hall to his room and T.J. couldn't help but wonder what he'd done to upset her this time. He couldn't think of anything, but he had every intention of finding out what was wrong once they had Seth settled down for the night.

"Good night, partner," T.J. said, when he placed the toddler in his tiny bed. "I'll see you in the morning."

"'Tory," the little boy said, yawning.

"I'll only be a few minutes," Heather said, picking up a book.

When T.J. started to leave the room, Seth sat up in bed and shook his head. "'Tory."

"I'm not real good with toddler-speak," T.J. said, frowning. "What does he want?"

"He wants you to stay for the story," she said, sighing heavily.

T.J. could tell Heather didn't want him hanging around for their nightly ritual, but he had a feeling that whether he left or he stayed, either way he was going to upset one of them. "Would you rather I go on into the living room to watch TV, Heather?"

She stared at him for a long moment before she shook her head. Then she sat down on a small chair beside the bed. "No, it's fine for you to stay." Opening the book, she added, "It won't take more than a couple of pages and he'll be asleep."

As she started reading about a little train named Thomas, T.J. watched her expressions and listened to the tone of her voice. Heather was a great mom and Seth was lucky to have her. She listened to her son, cared about what he wanted and tried to accommodate his wishes within reason. She was the kind of mother that any man would want for his children. The kind of mother T.J. would want for his kids.

His heart stalled. What the hell? He'd never even thought about having kids before. Was he actually thinking about that now?

When he noticed Seth's eyelids drift lower and lower until they closed completely, T.J. breathed a little easier. The sooner the little boy was sound asleep, the sooner he and Heather could go into the living room and he could regain his perspective.

Heather continued reading for another minute or two before she closed the book, stood up and turned off the lamp on the dresser. She followed T.J. from the room and closed the door behind them.

When they entered the living room, T.J. turned and put his hands on her shoulders. "What's wrong? And don't tell me nothing. You weren't this quiet when you were sick."

"Let's go into the kitchen," she suggested. "We can talk in there without disturbing Seth."

Nodding, he waited until they were both seated at the kitchen table before he asked, "What's going on, Heather?"

He watched her take a deep breath before she looked him square in the eye. "After the road clears and you're able to get back to your ranch, I'd rather you not come over here anymore."

"Why? Was it because of that kiss this afternoon?" He had figured they would get around to discussing it sooner or later. But he had hoped that talking about it would lead to more kisses. If the determined expression on her pretty face was any indication, it didn't appear it was headed that way.

"Yes and no," she said slowly.

"Would you care to explain that?" Besides the kiss, he couldn't think of anything else he'd done that could have upset her to this degree.

"I don't want you to take offense to what I'm about to tell you," she said, choosing her words carefully. "But I don't want you around Seth anymore."

Of all the grievances he might have expected her to have with him, not wanting him to interact with her son wasn't among them.

"Why don't you tell me how I'm supposed to take it?" he demanded, suddenly angry. "As far as I know, Seth and I have been getting along just fine. I've even made sure to watch my language around him because I didn't want him picking up words you'd rather he didn't learn."

She nodded. "And I appreciate your vigilance on that."

T.J. folded his arms and leaned back in his chair. "Then what's the deal, Heather? Why am I good enough to look after him one minute, but not the next?"

"I'm trying to protect my son from becoming too attached to you," she explained. "I don't want to see him get hurt."

T.J.'s anger hit the boiling point. Unfolding his arms,

he sat forward and pointed his finger at her. "Let's get one thing straight right here and now, Heather Wilson. I would never do or say anything to cause you or Seth any kind of harm— physically or emotionally. I'm not that kind of guy and I never will be."

"I know you wouldn't mean to," she said, shaking her head. She looked vulnerable and upset. "But children hold nothing back. When they care for someone, they give their love and trust unconditionally because they don't know any other way. They don't realize that because someone is in their life now that the person might not always be there. I can see he likes you and he wants you around, but I'm afraid he'll start to depend on you to be there for him. Then when you aren't, when you get tired of us, he won't understand."

T.J. stared at her for several long moments. Seth wasn't the only one she was trying to protect. She might not realize it, but Heather was afraid of being hurt emotionally, as well. Given all that she had lost, he could understand her caution. But he could tell by the stubborn set of her chin that she had her mind made up. Trying to convince her of the flaw in her reasoning at this point in time would be nothing more than wasted energy.

Even though he hated to give in, he said, "It's your call." He shrugged as he rose from the chair. He motioned toward the living room. "If you don't mind, I think I'll watch the news and turn in. I assume it's all right for me to stretch out on the couch?"

A shadow of disappointment briefly crossed her pretty face, verifying what he suspected. She was afraid she would start to count on him, to want him to be around. What she didn't realize—and what he wasn't going to point out—was that she had already started depending on him. She already wanted him to be a part of her and Seth's lives. Otherwise she wouldn't have been let down when T.J. hadn't argued with her about her decision.

"I'm sorry about you having to sleep on the couch," she said in apology, straightening her shoulders as she rose to her feet. "I closed off the upstairs to save on the heating bills, as well as wear and tear on a furnace that's older than I am."

"No problem," he said, following her to the hall closet. When she handed him a pillow and blanket their hands brushed and a jolt of yearning ran straight up his arm to settle in the middle of his chest. He did his best to ignore it.

"I'll see you tomorrow."

"Good night."

T.J. turned and walked into the living room, tossed the blanket and pillow on the couch, then sat down in one of the armchairs to stare blindly at some cop show on TV.

What the hell was going on? He wasn't looking to get tangled up with a woman, was he? So why the hell did Heather telling him to buzz off matter to him?

He should be relieved. Instead he was pissed off by her stubbornness and by what he believed to be her unreasonable fear that he would somehow cause her or Seth some kind of emotional pain.

As he stared at the TV, he pondered their conversation. He knew her reluctance stemmed from having lost the two most important men in her life in a relatively short period of time. She had to have felt completely abandoned and although she might not realize it, her current resistance to getting close to anyone was due to her fear that she could lose any new person in her life the way she had lost her father and fiancé.

Was he open to taking on that kind of emotional baggage?

They certainly had an abundance of chemistry between them. They couldn't be within ten feet of each other without him wanting to take her in his arms. And if her reaction to him was any indication, she wanted to be there.

So what did he intend to do about it?

He really didn't think he had ever been in a real relationship. There were women he'd dated, but he had been so focused on his goal of winning world championships in bronc riding events and then buying a ranch and building his breeding program that he hadn't been serious about any of them.

In his rodeo days, he'd spent time with some of the buckle bunnies who hung around hoping to add another rider's name to the list of cowboys they'd bedded who had earned championship belt buckles. He wasn't overly proud of his past, but his name had been added to several of those bunnies' lists. And, of course, whenever he had an overwhelming urge for female companionship, he'd made his share of trips over to the Broken Spoke in Beaver Dam to find a warm, willing woman who didn't want anything more from him than one night and a real good time. But he had never committed himself to any kind of exclusive or serious relationship with a woman, especially not a woman with a child in tow.

Heather wasn't the type of woman a man took to bed and then walked away from the following morning without so much as a backward glance. She was part of a package deal. She had a cute little kid. Any man who entered into a relationship with her would be in a relationship with her little boy, as well. Was T.J. even thinking about trying to make that kind of connection with Heather? What if things didn't work out? He certainly didn't want to hurt Seth if they didn't.

T.J. turned off the television and removed his boots, got up from the chair and stretched out on the couch. As he lay there, trying to ignore the obviously broken spring poking him in the middle of his back, he knew exactly what he was going to do and why he was so damned frustrated.

Heather was more than just a single mother who was barely making ends meet and had no one to turn to for help. She was the only woman who had piqued his interest this much in a very long time—maybe ever. He just couldn't walk away from that. If he did, he had a feeling he would regret it for the rest of his life. His instincts had served him well over the years and he wasn't about to start questioning them now.

Whether she liked it or not, she would have to get used to the fact that he wasn't going anywhere. She needed someone to turn to if things got rough or slipped out of her control. And T.J. intended to be there for both her and Seth.

Now all he had to do was convince her to give him a chance. And he intended to get started on that first thing in the morning.

Five

The following morning, Heather woke up to find the pillow and blanket she had given T.J. the night before stacked neatly on the end of the couch, but he was no-where in sight. As she continued on into the kitchen, she looked out the window over the sink to see if his truck was still parked next to her car. It wasn't.

When a keen sense of disappointment washed over her, she tried to remind herself that this was the way she wanted it—the way it had to be. She should be happy that he hadn't argued with her, that he'd done what she'd asked.

But she wasn't.

She had spent a miserable night going over all of the reasons why she'd asked T.J. to stay away from her and her son. Surely that was the only way to ensure that Seth didn't get hurt.

But reasoning with herself didn't do a thing to stop the abject loneliness that seemed to go all the way to her soul.

Sighing, she turned to get a mug from the cabinet. That's when she noticed a note on the counter in front of a freshly made pot of coffee. T.J. let her know that he had tended to the horses. He'd thanked her for giving him a place to stay for the night and told her to get in touch with him if she needed anything.

"Well, it looks like you accomplished what you set out to do," she muttered to herself as she poured a cup of coffee and started a pan of oatmeal for her son's breakfast.

So why didn't she feel better about it?

"Mom-mom, hungee," Seth said sleepily as he toddled into the room.

"I'm making your favorite, sweetie. Oatmeal with cinnamon and a sprinkle of brown sugar," she said, picking him up.

"Hossy?" he asked, looking around the kitchen.

"T.J. had to go home," she said gently.

"No!" Seth shook his little head. "My hossy."

"Maybe we'll see T.J. another time," she offered, hoping the thought would be enough to keep Seth from becoming more upset.

Luckily, it did seem to pacify him for a while, but he did ask about T.J. periodically throughout the morning and by the time she got Seth down for his nap after lunch, Heather felt as if she could cry. It was clear that

Seth missed T.J. and if she was honest with herself, she did, too.

How could the man have integrated himself into their lives in such a short amount of time? And what was there about him that was so darned compelling?

He wasn't the first man who had shown her attention since she'd found herself on her own.

One of the ranchers from the next county over had bought one of her brood mares last year. Several months ago, he had come by to take her and Seth for ice cream on the pretense of discussing the purchase of another horse. It had quickly become apparent that he considered the outing a date. Although he was nice enough, the kiss he'd given her when he'd brought them home had done nothing to encourage her to go anywhere else with him. She compared that to the first time T.J. had kissed her. That had felt as if time stood still. It had left her wanting him to do it again, and soon.

She rubbed at the tension building between her eyes. Why him? Why did T. J. Malloy have to be the one to awaken a need in her that she had all but forgotten?

When she'd told him that she was concerned for Seth, concerned about the bond she could see growing between them, she had deliberately omitted the fact that she was frightened by the way he made her feel, as well. T.J. reminded her of how much she missed being in a relationship, of how lonely life was without someone to share it with.

Of course, he had talked about being a good neighbor and wanting to help her with the ranch, but beyond kissing her a few times he hadn't mentioned anything about a relationship. And she wasn't interested in one, either.

Was she?

As she sat at the kitchen table, wondering if the stress had finally gotten to her and she'd lost what little sense she had left, Heather heard a vehicle coming up the driveway. When she glanced out the window, two white trucks with the Dusty Diamond logo painted on the sides, followed by T.J.'s black truck, parked close to the barn. The beds of the trucks were all piled high with bales of hay, straw and sacks of grain.

She wasn't certain whether she was happy to see T.J. or angry that he had ignored her request not to stop by again. A mixture of emotions coursed through her when he got out of his truck. Even from a distance he was so darned good-looking it was almost sinful, but he apparently had ignored everything she'd told him.

She started to go outside to see what he thought he was doing, but when she glanced at the clock she realized Seth would be waking up soon. Not wanting to get him up before his nap was over and unwilling to leave him alone in the house, she stepped out onto the porch to call out to T.J. "Would you please come up to the house for a few minutes?"

When he walked across the ranch yard and up the steps, just the sight of him was enough to take her breath away, which seemed to happen too frequently around him. But when he stopped in front of her and gave her a brief kiss on the lips, she wondered if she would ever breathe again.

"What's up, sweetheart?"

His easy smile sent a shiver of longing straight up her spine and she forgot all about admonishing him for kissing her and for not staying away liked she'd asked.

"Wh-where did all that come from?" she asked, pointing to the supplies his men were unloading and carrying into her barn. It was much easier to focus on what he had done than on the man himself. "I can't pay for it. I only buy what I can afford."

He shook his head. "Don't worry about it. I had some extra hay and straw taking up space in my loft. The other day when my foreman ordered oats, he ordered several dozen extra bags. I thought you might as well have them. It'll save you from having to make a trip to town in the next day or so."

"I told you I'm not a charity case," she said, shaking her head.

He had the audacity to ignore her. "Where's the little cowboy?"

"He's taking a nap," she answered automatically. "Tell your men to stop unloading those supplies and take them back to your place."

Cupping her elbow in one hand, he turned her, opened the door and escorted her into the house. "That's not going to happen, Heather. I owe you and I've let this debt go long enough."

She frowned. "What are you talking about? You don't owe me anything."

He nodded. "Yes, I do. You have a champion stallion that bred at least eight of my mares over the past couple of years. I never paid the stud fees."

"Have you lost your mind?" she demanded. "Up until yesterday, you thought Magic Dancer was an unregistered rogue stallion who had done serious damage to your breeding program."

"I found out differently," he said, shrugging. He removed his jean jacket and pulled out a chair. Then he sat down at the table as if it was his right. He motioned for her to join him at the table.

"Have a seat. We need to talk."

She remained standing. "About?"

"Sit and I'll tell you," he answered.

"Do you always have to have your way?" she asked as she took the chair across from him. "I thought I made myself clear last night about—"

"We'll discuss your edict a little later." She had seen that look of determination on his handsome face before—the evening when he'd insisted she and Seth spend another night at his ranch. "Right now, I want to tell you something and I want you to promise that you'll wait until I'm finished before you comment."

Heather wasn't certain remaining silent would be in her best interest, but it was apparent he wasn't going to tell her what he had on his mind until she gave her word she wouldn't interrupt.

She sighed heavily. "All right."

"After I take care of your horses tomorrow—"

"I told you I would take care of my own horses from now on," she insisted.

Instead of reminding her of her promise not to interrupt, he simply tilted his head slightly and gave her a smile that clearly stated he had known she couldn't keep her comments to herself.

"Oh, all right," she said, folding her arms beneath her breasts. "Finish what you were going to tell me."

"Like I was saying, after I tend to the horses tomorrow, one of my men and I are going to go up on the roof and check to see what it will take to keep it from leaking." When she started to tell him she wouldn't allow it, he held up his hand. "Hear me out. We'll only do a patch job that will hopefully get you through until spring. Is that the only area that's been leaking?"

"Yes, but—"

"Okay, we'll give it a quick fix to get you through the rest of the winter, then you can see about having that section reroofed when the weather warms up."

He sat back in the chair as if he was quite proud of himself.

"Are you finished?" she asked. When he nodded, she shook her head. "I can't let you climb on top of my house and run the risk of falling off."

To her surprise he threw back his head and laughed. "Sweetheart, I appreciate your concern for my safety, but I know what I'm doing when it comes to roofing houses. From the time I graduated high school until I graduated from college, I spent every summer roofing houses during the week while I rode rodeo on the weekends to earn money for school."

"I don't care. I'm not going to let you do that," she insisted. "I wouldn't feel right about you fixing my roof without compensation and right now I can't pay for it. And while we're talking about things I can't pay for, you might as well tell your men to load those supplies back on your trucks and return them to the Dusty Diamond because I can't pay for those, either."

"I thought we already had that settled," he said, getting up to walk around the table. Before she knew what he was up to, he scooped her up, sat down in her chair and settled her on his lap. "The supplies are for the stud fees I owe you for your horse breeding my mares. End of discussion." He kissed the side of her neck. "And my men and I *will* be fixing your roof tomorrow. If you want to make lunch for us, we'll call it even. Once again, end of discussion."

How was she supposed to protest when she couldn't even think with him holding her, kissing her? And why was she unable to resist when he picked her up to set her on his lap?

She wasn't sure. But every time he held her like this, she not only felt the chemistry between them, but a calm also came over her, as if she'd found a safe haven from all the responsibilities she'd faced for the past two and a half years.

"And just so you know, last night when you told me you didn't want me around, you misunderstood my silence as agreeing that I would do what you wanted," he said, nibbling kisses from her neck to the hollow beneath her ear. "That wasn't the case, sweetheart. I'm not going anywhere. I want to help you out. I want to make things easier for you and Seth."

"I don't think you being around will do anything but make things more difficult and complicated for us," she said honestly.

He cupped her cheek with his palm and held her gaze with his. "There's something going on between you and me, Heather. Whatever is drawing us together—I know it makes you as frightened for yourself as you are afraid of Seth being hurt. And to tell you the truth, I'm unsettled by this pull between us, too. But I gave it a lot of thought last night and I decided we can't ignore it. It exists, whether we like it or not. But I give you my word that I'll walk through hell before I hurt you or Seth."

"We should try to ignore it," she insisted, unable to sound as convincing as she would have liked, even to herself. She didn't try to deny that there was a definite chemistry between them. They'd both know she was lying.

"I'm not willing to do that," he said firmly as he lowered his head.

The moment his lips settled over hers, Heather gave up trying to fight with herself and closed her eyes. She might not be the least bit comfortable with it, but she wanted T.J.'s kiss. She wanted him to make her feel that she was more than just a single mom, struggling to make ends meet on a ranch that was quickly slipping through her grasp. She wanted him to make her feel like a woman again.

When he coaxed her mouth to open for him, he slipped his tongue inside to tease her into playing a game of advance and retreat. Heat flowed from the top of her head all the way to the soles of her feet. She felt a strong sense of feminine power course through her when he encouraged her to take control and explore him the way he had explored her.

She brought her hand up so she could tangle her fingers in the soft curls at the nape of his neck. His arms tightened around her. When her nails lightly chafed his skin, a groan rumbled up from deep in his chest. That's when she became aware of his rapidly growing arousal pressing against her hip. Her own body responded with a delicious warmth that gathered in the most feminine part of her, and she couldn't stop herself from melting against him.

"Hossy!" she heard Seth squeal as he ran into the kitchen.

The warmth flowing through her veins quickly cooled. Pulling back, she looked at T.J. to see if he was angered that the kiss had been called to such an abrupt halt. His understanding smile surprised her. A lot of men would have resented someone else's child interrupting a passionate embrace. But T.J. seemed to be taking it in stride.

"We'll continue this later," he promised Heather, kissing the tip of her nose. Turning his attention to Seth, T.J. grinned as he reached down with one arm to pick up her son. "Hey there, little partner. Did you have a nice nap?"

"Yesh," Seth said, throwing his arms around T.J.'s neck to hug him. "Wide hossy."

"You'll have to ask your mom," T.J. said, laughing.

"Pease, Mom-mom?"

Her son looked so hopeful she couldn't say no.

"Just one and then we'll have to let T.J. get back to helping his men," she said as she got up from T.J.'s lap.

"Otay." Seth's little grin melted her heart.

Her little boy meant everything to her, but T.J. was right. Whatever this was between the two of them couldn't be ignored. She just hoped she wasn't setting up Seth—or herself—for an emotional fall.

But as she watched T.J. get down on his hands and knees to give Seth a ride around the kitchen, she realized that whatever force of nature was drawing her and T.J. together, it included her son, too. Seth wasn't a child who easily warmed up to strangers, but he had immediately gravitated toward T.J. And T.J. didn't seem to mind in the least. In fact, watching the two together was like watching a father playing with his son.

Her breath caught in her throat and she had to force herself not to panic. She had always heard that it took a special man to accept another man's child as his own. Was T.J. really that kind of man?

Thus far, he had been extraordinary. He hadn't hesitated one bit to help her with Seth and if he saw that she needed something, whether she wanted him to or not, he did his best to take care of it for her. He was the kind of man she would want to be a father to her son.

She shook her head to dispel the thought that he could be a father to Seth and reminded herself to take things one day at a time. Nothing had been said about a relationship and T.J. had promised that he wouldn't cause Seth any kind of harm, not even emotionally. But could she take it on faith that T.J. wasn't just telling her what she wanted to hear? She'd had so many disappointments in the past couple of years, it was hard for her to trust that everything would work out.

"Okay, partner, time for me to go see if my crew has everything unloaded and put away in the barn," T.J. said, stopping to let Heather lift Seth from his back.

"What do you say, Seth?" Heather prompted.

"Tank 'ou," he said, smiling.

"You're welcome, partner," T.J. said as he rose to his feet.

Holding her son with one arm, Heather reached for T.J.'s jacket with the other. "I'm still not comfortable with all of this," she said quietly as she handed him the jacket.

"We've already settled everything, sweetheart." He took his jacket from her, pulled it on and wrapped his arms around both her and Seth. "We'll take things one day at a time and see where each day takes us." He checked his watch. "I wish I could hang around, but I got a call from one of my brothers after I got home this morning. I'm supposed to meet him over in Beaver Dam for supper."

"You don't owe me any kind of explanation," she said, shaking her head. "I wasn't even expecting you to come by today."

"I just wanted you to know where I'd be in case you need me for anything," he said, kissing her forehead as he handed her a business card with the Dusty Diamond logo printed on it, along with his cell number.

"Seth and I will be just fine," she assured him, tucking the card into her jeans pocket.

"Then I'll see you tomorrow," he said, stepping back to head for the door.

As she watched T.J. leave the house, Heather felt as if she had just jumped off into the deep end of a pool with no idea how to swim. Was she really going to let T.J. help her? Was she really going to go along with his idea that they needed to explore their attraction?

Watching him from the kitchen, she saw him talk to his men then turn to wave to her as he got into his truck. Heather's heart skipped a beat and she nibbled nervously on her lower lip. Just the thought of becoming involved with anyone scared her beyond words.

Her child deserved a father—a man who would love him, play with him and teach him things. But could a man still care for another man's child once he had one of his own? Did that kind of man even exist?

Her father had been one of the finest men she had ever known and he hadn't been able to do it. Her older sister had been the child of their mother's first marriage and from what she had discerned from Stephanie's comments, everything had been fine until Heather was born. After that, her father doted on Heather and no longer seemed to have enough time for her sister. She didn't want to see the same thing happen to her son.

But whether it was smart or not, it appeared that she had already become involved with T.J., and her son had started looking to him as a father figure, even if he was too young to realize it.

When T.J. spotted Lane at the back of the Broken Spoke, he stopped at the bar for a bottle of beer before walking over to slide into the seat on the opposite side of the wide booth. Taking off his hat, he hung it on one of the pegs on the wall.

"What did you do to piss off Taylor this time?" he asked, unable to keep from grinning.

Lane frowned. "What makes you think my wife is mad at me?"

"Since the two of you got married last spring, I can count on one hand the number of times you've gone anywhere without her," T.J. replied. "And if my memory serves me right, both of those times you had done something that caused her to pitch a hissy fit and you wanted to give her the time and space to cool off."

T.J. had decided as soon as he met Taylor that the fiery redhead was perfect for Lane. Her passion and enthusiasm for life tempered Lane's tendency to be overly serious and analytical, while his calm lessened her propensity to overreact.

"Well, I didn't do anything this time," his brother said, shaking his head. "She's not been feeling very well the past couple of days."

"Does she have the flu?" T.J. asked, hoping that wasn't the case. "That's what Hea—" He coughed to cover his blunder. "That's what I've heard is going around."

"No, she's got some kind of stomach bug," Lane said, obviously missing T.J.'s slip of the tongue. "Since she doesn't feel like cooking and doesn't want to do anything but sleep, I figured I'd let her rest and see if you and the other guys wanted to grab a steak."

"Who else is coming?" T.J. asked.

"I think Ryder and Sam are headed this way." Lane took a swig of his beer, then laughed. "Sam said, after Bria gets little Hank down for the night, she and Mariah are going to experiment with hairstyles for Mariah's big night in Dallas with her new boyfriend. And Ryder said that Summer told him if he didn't stop hovering over her and the baby, she was going to bop him."

T.J. laughed. "I can't say I blame Sam for not wanting to hang around for the hairstyling. And as protective as Ryder is, I'm surprised he hasn't covered both Summer and the baby in bubble wrap."

Grinning, Lane nodded. "Can you imagine what Ryder will eventually put some poor, pimple-faced boy through when the kid comes around trying to date Katie?"

"What do you want to bet Ryder makes sure he's cleaning one of his guns when the kid comes to pick her up?" T.J. asked, feeling sorry for whoever dared to ask out his niece.

"Yeah, he'll intimidate the stuffing out of the kid," Lane agreed.

"But you'll have to admit, the boy will think twice before trying anything out of line with Katie," T.J. added. "By the way, have you talked to Jaron since Mariah made her announcement Christmas night?" he asked, knowing their brother hadn't been happy to hear the news that she was seeing someone.

"When I called to ask him to join us tonight, I tried to talk to him about it." Lane shrugged. "He told me to mind my own business and said he had something else he had to do."

T.J. nodded. "You know how he is. He's not much on talking about his troubles. He tends to brood about things that are bothering him more than the rest of us do."

"Yeah," Lane agreed. "But until he's ready, it doesn't do any good to try to draw him out."

"Nope." T.J. took a long draw of his beer. "Jaron knows where to find us when he's ready to talk."

"There's Sam and Ryder," Lane said, pointing toward the bar's front door.

As T.J. watched his brothers make their way to the booth, he slid to the far side for one of them to sit down. When Sam and Ryder joined them, T.J. asked, "What about Nate? Is he going to be here?"

Lane shrugged. "He said he was heading to Waco this evening."

"He really needs to marry that girl and get it over with." Ryder was only saying what they were all thinking.

"He told me the other night that they broke up again," T.J. commented. "Right before he tried to give me advice on women."

They all laughed.

"And who was he trying to give you advice about?" Sam asked. "The only woman I know of that you've been seeing on a semi-regular basis is that neighbor of yours with the stallion."

T.J. almost choked on his beer. He knew that if his brothers got wind that he had been over at Heather's more than he'd been home for the past couple of days, they would never let him hear the end of it. But he wasn't sure how he could answer Sam without lying to him. And that's one thing he refused to do. He had never been dishonest with his brothers about anything and he wasn't going to start now.

Shrugging, he tried to be evasive. "He was telling me that I mishandled the situation with Hea—that Wilson woman about her horse."

"Whoa!" Ryder exclaimed.

Lane raised an eyebrow and slowly set his beer bottle on the table. "When did this come about, T.J.?"

He knew feigning ignorance wasn't going to stop the coming interrogation, but he tried anyway. "What?"

"You seeing your neighbor," Sam answered.

"Who said I've been seeing her?" he asked defensively. It was the first time he had been in the hot seat with his brothers over a woman and he suddenly knew how Sam, Ryder and Lane felt when they were the ones being counseled about their relationships.

"Any time we've mentioned her before you've always gone ballistic about her and her horse," Ryder stated flatly.

"I've let that go," T.J. said.

Sam shook his head. "I'm not buying it. The other night over at my place your reaction was as strong as ever. What's happened in the past few days that's changed your mind about her?"

"What makes you think something happened?" T.J. asked, knowing that he was only delaying the inevitable. His brothers weren't going to give up until they found out what was going on with him and Heather.

"The fact that you're answering every question we

ask with one of your own is a pretty good clue," Lane said, his smile about as irritating as any T.J. had ever seen.

"Is that your expert opinion, Freud?" T.J. retorted.

Lane laughed. "Yup."

"Fess up, bro," Ryder said, grinning like a damned jackass.

Blowing out a frustrated breath, T.J. gave in and explained about finding Heather and Seth stranded on his side of the creek Christmas night.

"They were both sick and I couldn't leave them sitting along the side of the road to fend for themselves," T.J. said, shaking his head. "Hank would come back from the grave to haunt me."

His three brothers nodded their agreement. Their foster father had instilled a keen sense of what was right and what wasn't. Leaving a woman in distress without helping her out of whatever situation she found herself in was an unforgivable sin. No exceptions.

"Did you know she had a kid when you were giving her such a hard time about that horse?" Ryder demanded.

"No." T.J. shook his head. "I wouldn't have been so demanding if I'd known she was trying to juggle taking care of a baby and running the Circle W by herself."

"Where's the little boy's daddy?" Sam asked. "Can't he lend a hand?"

Filling them in on what Heather had told him about losing her father and her fiancé just a few months apart, T.J. left out how much she was struggling. His brothers didn't need to know how hard she was finding it to make ends meet. For one thing, he had to consider her pride. She hadn't liked having to tell *him* and he didn't figure she would appreciate him discussing her business with his brothers. And for another, they had probably already figured it out for themselves.

"You're going to continue helping her out, aren't you?" Sam asked, his know-it-all smile almost as irritating as Lane's.

"I owe her," T.J. said, nodding. "It turns out that stud of hers is a registered quarter horse and a multi-champion horse in the pleasure class."

"And you thought he'd screwed up your breeding program," Lane said thoughtfully. "While in fact, he might have improved it."

Ryder laughed. "Funny how jumping to conclusions can come back to bite you in the butt."

"Shut up, smart-ass," T.J. muttered, wishing he'd skipped having supper with his brothers.

"What can I get for you guys?" a young, ponytailed waitress asked as she walked up to the booth. Snapping her chewing gum, she smiled as she added, "Our special tonight is a T-bone steak smothered in onions and green peppers with sides of French fries and coleslaw."

"Sounds good to me," Sam said.

"Make that two of the specials," Ryder agreed.

"How about you, T.J.?" Lane asked. When he nodded, Lane turned back to the girl. "Looks like we'll all have tonight's special, medium rare and add another round of beer to that order."

The girl nodded. "I'll be back with your beer in just a minute."

T.J. was relieved that once she left, the conversation turned to other things. By the time they finished dinner and got ready to leave, they all agreed they needed to get together for a brothers' night out more often.

"I guess I'll see all of you in a couple of days at the Dusty Diamond," T.J. said, reaching for his hat.

"We'll be there. Be prepared to help me carry in all the baby stuff we'll have to bring for Katie." Ryder laughed. "Going anywhere with a baby is like moving."

Sam nodded. "You got that right. It is getting a little better now that little Hank is almost a year old. But damn, even a trip to town can be a major undertaking."

"We'll be there if Taylor feels up to it," Lane said, nodding.

"She called Bria this afternoon and asked if Bria could handle making the dinner and the snacks they'd planned for our New Year's Eve party by herself," Sam said, looking concerned. "Have you taken Taylor to the doctor?"

"She has an appointment tomorrow afternoon," Lane said as they all stood up.

"Maybe he can give her something to get rid of whatever's making her feel bad," T.J. offered when they stopped to pay their checks at the bar.

"Let us know what the doctor has to say," Ryder added. As they walked out to the parking lot, he asked, "So are you going to invite your neighbor to the party, T.J.?"

"You really should," Sam said, grinning. "If you two are going to continue seeing each other, she might as well meet us now and see what she's up against."

"I'll think about it," T.J. muttered as he waved good-bye to his brothers and got into his truck.

On the drive home, he thought about what his brothers had said. He had entertained the idea of asking Heather and Seth to join the annual New Year's Eve party, but he hadn't had a chance to weigh the pros and cons of having her meet his family.

It wasn't that he thought they wouldn't welcome her or that she wouldn't fit in. He knew for a fact they would accept her and Seth with open arms and he was pretty sure Heather would become instant friends with all of his sisters-in-law. So why was he holding back?

He had talked to Heather about exploring what was drawing them together, but beyond that he hadn't mentioned anything about pursuing a relationship. Would it even be wise to introduce her to his family before they were even dating? What if nothing came of their seeing each other?

Turning his truck onto the lane leading up to his house, T.J. knew what he was going to do. Besides the fact that he wanted to spend time with her, he couldn't stand the thought of Heather and Seth sitting over in the Circle W ranch house by themselves while he and his family had a good old time seeing in the New Year together. But he knew it wouldn't be easy to convince her to join them.

He couldn't help but smile as he drove the truck into the garage. Fortunately he was up for the challenge.

Six

T.J. positioned the extension ladder he had brought from his ranch against the side of Heather's house, then walked back to his truck for one of the buckets of roof patch he'd had his foreman pick up at the local hardware store the day before. As soon as Tommy Lee finished taking care of Heather's horses, he would work with T.J. to fix the roof. Then T.J. intended to talk to her about the New Year's Eve party at his place the following night.

"T.J.?" Heather called from the porch. When he stepped around the corner of the house to see what she wanted, she was coming down the steps holding Seth's hand. "I'm sorry to bother you, but when Seth found out you were outside he insisted he had to see you."

T.J. grinned. "Hey there, partner."

"Hi!" Seth said, grinning from ear to ear. As soon as they stepped off the bottom step, Seth pulled his hand from Heather's and ran toward T.J.

Bending, T.J. caught the toddler in his arms. "How are you today?"

Seth's excited rapid-fire answer and the waving of his hands had T.J. looking to Heather for an interpretation.

"He's trying to tell you about helping me make lunch for you and your hired hand," she said, walking up to them.

"I'll bet you were a big help for your mom," T.J. said, smiling. "What did you help her fix up for us?"

"Scetti balls," Seth said proudly.

T.J. glanced at Heather. "Spaghetti and meatballs?" When she nodded, he tickled Seth's stomach, causing the toddler to burst into a fit of giggles. "We've had that before, haven't we, partner?"

Seth nodded. "You house."

"That's right," T.J. agreed, laughing. "You ate almost as much as I ended up wearing." When he spotted Tommy Lee walking out of the barn, T.J. set the little boy on his feet. "Time for me to fix the roof, but I'll be in as soon as I'm finished to eat lunch with you and give you another ride. How does that sound?"

"Please be careful," Heather said as she took Seth by the hand.

"Hey, where do you think you're going?" T.J. asked, stepping forward to wrap his arms around her waist.

She looked confused. "I thought you were going up on the roof."

"Not without a kiss," he said as he pressed his lips to hers. With Seth hanging around nearby, T.J. made sure to keep the kiss brief. When he lifted his head, he stared at Heather for several long seconds. She was so damned beautiful, it was all he could do to keep from kissing her until they both collapsed from lack of oxygen. "To be continued in the very near future."

"We'll be inside," she replied softly. "Come on in when you two get done."

As he watched her turn and lead Seth back into the house, he took a deep breath and waited for Tommy Lee. "Once I get up on the roof, all you have to do is hand me the bucket of roof patch."

"Fair enough, boss," the man said, looking relieved. "I'm not all that gung ho on heights."

"You climb up in the barn loft all the time," T.J. said as they walked around to the side of the house where he had put the ladder.

"I never said it didn't bother me," Tommy Lee admitted.

"I'll tell Dan to send Harry up there from now on," T.J. said, starting to climb up the ladder. When he reached the roof, he turned for the bucket. "You don't have any kind of problem with needles do you?"

"Nope." Tommy Lee handed T.J. the patching material. "Why?"

"Because Harry breaks out in a cold sweat every time he thinks about having to help the veterinarian," T.J. answered. "From now on you can help inoculate the horses."

"Sounds good to me," Tommy Lee said as he

climbed back down the ladder. "Funny that Harry never mentioned that."

"Did you tell him about your problem with heights?" T.J. asked, opening the bucket.

"Not on your life," Tommy Lee said. There was a pause before the young cowboy spoke again. "Oh, I get it."

T.J. couldn't help but grin as he started smearing the black, tar-like substance over the damaged spots on the roof. Tommy Lee's naiveté came more from being a twenty-year-old kid and out on his own for the first time than from anything else.

Just as T.J. finished with the last spot showing signs of damage, Tommy Lee let loose with a curse that raised even T.J.'s eyebrows.

"Get down here now, boss," the young man shouted. "Ms. Wilson's house is on fire."

Making his way across the roof to the ladder, T.J. could see thick gray smoke coming from the open window below. He repeated Tommy Lee's creative combination of cuss words and added a few of his own as he came down the ladder in what had to be record time. He ran around to the back of the house, followed closely by the younger cowboy. T.J. threw open the door and they met Heather carrying Seth as she ran through the kitchen to get out.

"I turned it off, but I think the furnace is on fire," she said.

"Get them out of here," he ordered Tommy Lee.

While his hired hand got Heather and Seth to safety, T.J. grabbed the fire extinguisher he had seen in a utility closet the night he'd stayed with Heather and entered the laundry room. He pulled the lever on top, sprayed foam on the furnace's smoldering motor and didn't stop until the small cylinder was empty. He wanted to make sure there was no chance of flames flaring up again before he went outside to see that Heather and Seth were all right.

"What happened?" he asked when he exited the house. He walked across the yard to where Heather stood, cradling Seth, and took them both into his arms.

"I-I'm not sure," she said, shivering against him. "I heard a pop and then smelled smoke. When I went to see what happened, smoke was coming from the furnace. I turned it off and opened the window, but the smoke just kept getting worse."

"Well, it's out now," he said, hugging her and Seth to him. "But I'm afraid your furnace motor is most likely a lost cause."

"That's…it. This…is the last…straw," she said haltingly. He could tell she was a hair's breadth away from dissolving into tears, and knowing how proud she was, he didn't think she would appreciate having an audience witnessing it.

"Tommy Lee, why don't you go ahead and put the bucket of roof patch in the tool shed, then take the ladder and go on back to the Dusty Diamond," T.J suggested. He'd intended to stay after lunch to talk to Heather about attending the family's New Year's Eve party, and now he was glad he had the young cowboy follow him over to Heather's in one of the ranch trucks.

"Will do, boss," Tommy Lee said, looking relieved to be escaping the coming waterworks.

"Why don't we get you and Seth out of this chilly air?" he asked, turning her toward the house. He lifted Seth from her and put his free arm around her shoulders to guide her up the steps and through the open back door.

Once they were inside, Heather turned into him and he held her while she sobbed against his chest. He'd rather climb a barbed-wire fence buck-naked than to see a woman cry, but Heather's tears made him feel worse than any he'd ever witnessed. He wanted to help, but he wasn't sure she would let him. He had barely convinced her to allow him to tend to her horses and fix her roof. Getting her to let him replace the furnace, or even just get it repaired, would be next to impossible.

"M-Mom-mom?" Seth said, his little voice wobbling.

Great! T.J. was going to have a sobbing woman and a crying toddler all at the same time.

"Your mom is going to be okay, Seth," he said, hoping to soothe the little boy. "I'll take good care of both of you. How does that sound?"

The child stared at him for a moment before he finally nodded. "O-tay."

When Heather's crying ran its course, T.J. reached for a soft cotton dish towel to dry her eyes. "Can you take Seth?" he asked. "I'm going to make a call to see if I can get a repairman out here right away."

"I-I'm so…sorry," she said, reaching for her son. "I never…cry."

"It's all right, sweetheart. This is just a little bump in the road and you're not going to face it alone." Cupping her face with his palms, he kissed her forehead. "Since it's supposed to be cold tonight, why don't you go ahead and start gathering some things for you and Seth to spend the night at my place? This late in the day, it's doubtful the furnace people will be able to get out here until tomorrow."

She stared at him for several long seconds before she drew in a deep breath. "Thank you, T.J."

He shook his head. "There's nothing to thank me for, Heather. I told you that I wanted to help you and make your life easier." He kissed her again. "And that's just what I'm going to do, sweetheart."

After dinner, Heather turned on the dishwasher and finished cleaning up T.J.'s kitchen before she started down the hall to join him and Seth in the game room. Fortunately, she'd had the presence of mind to bring the spaghetti and meatballs with them when she and Seth followed T.J. to the Dusty Diamond. Since it was already cooked, all she'd had to do was reheat it and she owed him at least one meal for patching her roof, making sure the burnt-out furnace motor hadn't caught the rest of the house on fire and the number of other things T.J. had done for her over the past several days.

A sudden wave of emotion threatened to overtake her, and she passed by the door to the game room and continued on to the powder room just a few feet away. Closing the door behind her, she took several deep breaths in an effort to chase away the tears she was

trying desperately not to shed. It was bad enough that
T.J. had witnessed her nerves getting the better of her
earlier in the day, she refused to allow him to see her
break down again.

What on earth was wrong with her? She hadn't been
this weepy since she was pregnant with Seth. That
could be blamed on hormonal changes and all that she
had lost during the pregnancy. But today?

Over the past two years, she had worked hard to
keep a positive attitude and not allow the stress to get
to her. And for the most part she had been successful.

She might have been able to deal with the furnace issues if she didn't also have the worry of finding money for the real estate taxes due at the end of
the next month. She had been over her meager budget time and again. Short of a miracle, it looked hope-
less. She could sell the rest of her brood mares to pay
for everything, but if she did that she wouldn't have
a breeding program left. She needed what money the
horses brought in to help keep everything else running
around the ranch.

When she told T.J. that the furnace breaking down
was the last straw, she had meant it. She couldn't afford
to replace it and if she couldn't pay the back taxes there
wouldn't be a reason to replace it anyway. The county
would seize the property and she and Seth would have
to find somewhere else to live.

Of course, if the furnace could be repaired, instead
of replaced, she might catch a bit of a break. When T.J.
called, the repairman had told him that he couldn't
come out to the Circle W until tomorrow morning to

assess the damage. But she didn't hold out a lot of hope that the solution would be that simple. The furnace was more than thirty years old and had been repaired so many times, it was probably a lost cause. But all the worry in the world wasn't going to change the outcome of the repairman's findings and she wasn't doing anyone any good making herself crazy over it.

She knew if she asked T.J. for help with her dilemma, he would be more than happy to do it. But there was no way her pride would allow her to do that. When she and her late fiancé first started dating, his parents had looked down on her because she was the daughter of a horse rancher, even though her parents had been far from destitute. They had gone so far as to accuse her of being more interested in the money their son would one day inherit than she was in him. She had vowed after that she would do without before she ever accepted help from anyone for anything. And although at times it had been extremely hard for her, she'd stuck to that vow. She saw no reason to go back on it now.

Taking a deep breath to calm herself, she splashed cold water on her face to erase some of the evidence of her panic then patted her skin dry. She left the powder room to join T.J. and Seth. She would just have to cling to the hope that things would work out.

"Why am I not surprised to see the two of you down on the floor again?" she asked, walking into the huge game room.

"Hossy," Seth said, happily patting T.J. on the top of the head.

T.J. laughed good-naturedly. "I think he's going to be a cowboy for sure."

"Why don't we let your horsey rest for a while?" Heather suggested, lifting Seth from T.J.'s back. "I'm sure his knees are getting sore from all the rides he's been giving you lately."

"Would you like something to drink?" T.J. asked, getting to his feet. He reached out to lightly run his finger along her cheek, sending shivers of anticipation coursing through her. "I've got soft drinks, beer and if you'd like, I could try to mix up one of those fruity drinks like a piña colada or a margarita." He grinned. "But I can't guarantee it will be any good. I'm a lot better at just opening a can or a bottle than I am at mixing up stuff."

Smiling, she had to catch her breath before she was able to speak. "Thank you, I'm fine. I need to let Seth play a little bit more, then give him a bath and get him settled down for the night."

"While you do that, I'll set up that little portable bed you brought with you," he offered as he pulled her to him for a quick kiss. "If you're not too tired, I'd like to talk to you about something after we get him in bed."

"All right," she said cautiously. "What do you want to discuss?"

"We'll talk about it later," he said, giving her a smile that caused her toes to curl inside her cross-trainers. Stepping back, he picked up Seth and headed toward the basket of toys he had mentioned keeping for his niece and nephew's visits. "Right now, I'm going to occupy my little partner here, while you put your feet up and relax for a while."

"You don't mind?" she asked.

He shook his head as he walked back over to her to brush her lips with his, then whispered close to her ear. "You need the break, sweetheart."

Tingles of excitement raced through her as Heather stared at him for a moment longer before she wandered over to the huge sectional sofa at the end of the room and sat down. Having help with Seth was a unique experience for her. Over the past two years, she had been so used to taking care of him on her own, she wasn't sure she even remembered how to relax.

As she sat there watching T.J. play with her son, she briefly wondered if this was the way it would have been if Seth's father had lived. Would he have been as helpful with their child as T.J. had been? Somehow, she doubted it. Although she knew Mike Hansen had loved her and would have adored Seth, he just hadn't been the thoughtful type.

A few minutes later, when she saw Seth yawn, she rose from the couch. "Time for a bath, sweetie."

"No," Seth said, frowning. "Wanna pway."

"I think we better listen to your mom," T.J. said, smiling. "She knows what's best."

Seth rubbed his eyes with both fists and shook his head. "Wanna pway."

"Tell you what, little partner." T.J. picked up her son and tickled his tummy. "I'll carry you upstairs for your bath and I promise we'll play again tomorrow. How does that sound?"

Heather's chest swelled with emotion when Seth threw his arms around T.J.'s neck to hug him. "Otay."

Although it frightened her to think that she might be setting them up for a tremendous amount of disappointment, she couldn't keep from being grateful for the attention T.J. had given Seth. In the past several days, it had been like watching a flower bloom. With T.J., Seth had opened up and become more talkative and outgoing than she could ever remember him being with anyone but her.

"Thank you," she said as they walked down the hall to the stairs.

T.J. put his free arm around her shoulders and drew her close. "For what?"

"For watching Seth and being so good with him," she answered.

"You've had a pretty rough day and I thought you could use a few minutes to catch your breath." His grin warmed her entire body. "And to tell you the truth, I'm having as much fun as he is. He's a great kid." As they entered the bedroom, T.J. handed her son to her and picked up the folded play yard she had brought for Seth to sleep in. "Now, while you give him a bath, I'll get this set up." T.J. leaned forward to kiss her. "I'll meet you in the man cave in about an hour for our little talk."

She had no idea what T.J. thought they needed to discuss and she wasn't entirely sure she wanted to know. What she was focused on—and what was far more unsettling than anything he could possibly say— was the excitement building inside of her at the thought of spending a little time alone with one of the sexiest, most remarkable men she had ever met.

While he waited for Heather to finish getting Seth to sleep, T.J. sat at the bar in his man cave drinking a beer and pondering how he could have gotten in so deep so damned fast. Whenever he was around Heather he couldn't seem to keep his hands off of her. All he wanted to do was hold her, kiss her—and do a whole lot more. And when he was away from her, he couldn't wait until they were together again.

Then there was her little boy. The time he spent with Seth was more special than T.J. would have imagined. The kid could melt rock with that cute grin of his and a couple of times T.J. had caught himself thinking about all of the things he could teach Seth when the boy got a little older.

He shook his head. Although he had no idea where they were headed and it definitely had him questioning his sanity, T.J. knew he couldn't turn back now. Come hell or high water, he would see this relationship through to the end, whether that came two months down the line or lasted an entire lifetime. If he didn't, he had a feeling he would end up regretting it for the rest of his life.

Hearing Heather enter the room, he turned to watch her and his heart stalled. She was without a doubt the most desirable woman he had ever seen.

"Do you have any idea how beautiful you are, Heather?" he asked.

When she walked over to where he sat on one of

the high-backed stools at the bar he didn't think twice about wrapping his arms around her and pulling her to him.

"I...um, never really thought a lot about being attractive," she said, her cheeks coloring a pretty pink.

She was clearly unused to receiving compliments and that was an oversight he intended to remedy every chance he got. "You are, sweetheart. You're also damned amazing in others ways, too." He nuzzled his cheek against the soft waves of her long strawberry blond hair. "You're a great mom and one of the strongest, most intelligent women I've ever known."

"Thanks, but what brought this on?" she asked, sounding delightfully breathless.

Leaning back to look into her brilliant blue eyes, he smiled. "I'm just stating the obvious."

"Is that what you wanted to talk to me about?" she asked, frowning. "You wanted to tell me that you think I'm amazing?"

Smiling, he pressed a kiss to her forehead. "Nope. But I do think you're amazing."

He rose from the bar stool and, after walking behind the bar to throw his empty beer bottle away, he took her by the hand and led her over to the sofa. As soon as they sat down, he watched her place an electronic receiver with a small video screen on the coffee table. He hadn't noticed her holding it, and when he looked closer he realized it was a baby monitor like the kind he had seen his sisters-in-law use for his niece and nephew.

"Now are you going to tell me what you wanted to discuss with me?" she asked.

Pulling her close, he smiled when she automatically brought her arms up to his shoulders and tangled her fingers in the hair at his nape. "We can get to what I want to talk about later," he said, lowering his head. "Right now, I'm going to do what I've been wanting to do all evening."

When he covered her mouth with his, T.J. reacquainted himself with her perfect lips. Soft and sweet, they were the kind of lips that a man couldn't resist and he didn't even intend to try. Instead he coaxed her to open for him. Teasing and exploring her with a thoroughness that instantly had him shifting to relieve the pressure building in his jeans, he laid her back on the wide couch without breaking contact.

Thankful that the sectional was extra wide, he stretched out with her. He half covered her body and his thigh came to rest against her feminine warmth. The moist heat radiating through the layers of their clothing sent his own temperature soaring and without a second thought, T.J. slid his hand from her back to her chest, cupping her full breast with his palm.

Her mint green T-shirt and bra quickly became intolerable barriers. Slipping his hand beneath the hem of the garment, he slid it up her abdomen to the valley between her breasts and unfastened the front clasp of the scrap of lace holding her captive. When he took the weight of her breast in his hand, his body burned from the feel of her satiny skin and hardened nipple. As he chafed the tight tip with the pad of his thumb,

Heather moaned softly and arched into his touch. The movement sent fire racing through his veins and as impossible as it seemed, his body tightened further. No matter what she'd said, no matter how hard she'd tried to push him away, he knew she wanted him as much as he wanted her. The thought was almost enough to send him spiraling out of control.

Breaking the kiss, he nibbled his way along her cheek to her temple. "Heather, I swear I only meant to kiss you," he said, his voice raspy with passion. "But I need you more right now than I need my next breath." He paused to raise his head and stare into her pretty blue eyes. "If you don't need me just as much, tell me now. Otherwise, I can almost guarantee you that we're going to make love." He kissed her soft, warm lips. "And when we do, I don't want you regretting one moment of what we share."

She stared at him for what felt like an eternity. "There are a lot of decisions I've made lately that I'm not sure of and some that I know I'll regret. I don't want to add—"

"I understand, sweetheart," he said, wondering if dead-lifting a horse or two would take care of the abundance of adrenaline coursing through him.

Removing his hand from her breast, he started to get up and head for the barn, but when Heather's arms tightened around his neck to hold him in place, he looked down at her and his heart started thumping against his ribs like a bass drum in a marching band. The desire he saw in her blue gaze was electrifying.

"Heather?"

"If you had let me finish, I was about to tell you that I don't want to add *not* making love with you to the list of things I'll regret," she said softly. "Tonight I want to forget about broken furnaces and wondering if I'm going to make ends meet from one day to the next. I don't want to worry about the future. Tonight I just want to feel."

His breath lodged in his lungs and it took a moment for him to draw in enough air to speak. "Are you sure, sweetheart?"

Nodding, she pressed her lips to his. "Yes."

Seven

Gazing up at T.J., Heather knew that she could very well be making the biggest mistake of her life, but she had never really had a choice. From the moment T.J. had kissed her that very first time in her kitchen, it had been leading up to this moment.

When he got up from the couch, he picked up the baby monitor, then held out his hand to help her to her feet. "Let's go upstairs to my room," he said, putting his arm around her shoulders to lead her toward the stairs. "We'll be more comfortable."

As they reached the top of the stairs, they stopped at the room she shared with her son to check on him sleeping soundly in the play yard before she and T.J. continued down the hall to the master suite. When he opened the door and turned on the bedside lamp using a switch by the door, he stepped back for her to enter ahead of him. She barely had time to notice that the room had a huge king-size bed, a wall of windows that seemed to make the star-studded night sky part of the room and that it was decorated in a rustic Western décor before he took her back into his arms.

"Sweetheart, I'm going to do my damnedest to take things slow," he said, raining tiny kisses from her lips to the hollow beneath her ear. "And I want you to promise that you'll let me know what feels good, what brings you the most pleasure."

Her heart raced at his intimate tone and her breathing became shallow due to his warm breath feathering over her sensitive skin. "It's been…quite a while."

"Since your fiancé?" he asked, bending to remove her shoes and his boots.

"Y-yes," she answered breathlessly when he caressed her foot and ankle as he removed her socks.

Removing his own, he straightened to take her hands in his. "We'll learn together how to please each other." His promising smile warmed her all over as he placed her palms on the front of his chambray shirt. "Why don't we start with you taking this off of me?"

Tugging the tail of the garment from the waistband of his jeans, she slowly released the snaps, then slid her hands inside the cloth to ease it from his wide, heavily muscled shoulders and down his bulging biceps. As the shirt fell to the floor, a shiver of excitement coursed through her at the sight of his well-developed torso.

"You're beautiful," she said, lightly touching the

thick pads of pectoral muscle. "Your muscles are so defined."

He shrugged. "It's a remnant from my rodeo days."

"Let me guess, you rode the rough stock," she said, glancing at the size of his upper arms. Every cowboy she had ever known who competed in those events had biceps most men would kill for. "Horses or bulls?"

"Bareback and saddle broncs," he said, smiling. "I also did a little team roping with my brother Lane when I first started out."

His smile faded and a shudder ran through his big body as she used her finger to trace each ridge and valley of his exceptional abs. By the time she reached his navel, a groan was rumbling up from deep in his chest. "You have no idea how good it feels to have you touch me like this," he said, his voice gruff with need.

"Probably as good as it felt when you touched me earlier on the couch," she admitted, wondering if that sultry female voice had really come from her.

He reached for the hem of her T-shirt to lift it up and over her head. Then, when he brushed her bra straps over her shoulders, she realized he hadn't refastened the clasp. But the thought was fleeting as he covered her breasts with his hands. The feel of his calloused palms chafing her taut nipples caused her to tremble with longing and her knees to feel as if they would give way.

When he lowered his head to kiss his way from her collarbone down the slope of her breast to the tight peak, Heather felt heat race through her veins to gather into a pool in the most feminine part of her. But when

T.J. took her nipple into his mouth to tease her with his tongue, she thought she would surely burn to a cinder.

"Does that feel good?" he asked as he moved to do the same to her other breast.

"Y-yes," she said, bracing her hands at his waist to steady herself.

He held her gaze with his as he slid his hands down her sides to her waistband, then made quick work of unbuttoning her jeans and slowly easing down the zipper. She took a deep breath and nodded, and he slipped the denim from her hips and down her legs. When she stepped out of the jeans, he took her in his arms. The feel of her breasts crushed to his hard chest sent a tiny electrical current skipping over every nerve ending in her body. It had been so long since she'd been desired by a man, since she had felt the heat and yearning of undeniable passion, that she briefly wondered how she had managed to keep her hands off of him as long as she had.

"O-one of us...is overdressed," she managed to say when she finally found her voice.

Stepping back, T.J. grinned. "I'd let you take care of getting rid of my jeans, but I think it would be better for me to do it this time." When he unbuttoned the waistband, then gingerly pulled the zipper down over the large bulge straining at his fly, Heather fully understood the reason for his caution. "Sometimes an erection and a zipper can be a painful combination," he said as he shoved the jeans down his long legs, then kicked them to the side.

When he started to remove his boxer briefs, she

smiled as she reached out to run her index finger along the top of the elastic waistband. "If you'd like, I can do that for you," she offered.

She watched him swallow hard a moment before he placed his hand at the top of her panties. "Why don't we do it together?"

When they lowered the last barriers between them, T.J. took a step back. "You're even more beautiful than I imagined," he said as his gaze seemed to touch every part of her.

"I was thinking the same thing about you," she said, memorizing every detail of his magnificent male body.

"As good as you look, I want to feel you against me," he said as he wrapped his arms around her and pulled her to him.

When their bodies met, it felt as if every nerve in her body tingled to life. She delighted in the contrast of her smooth feminine skin pressed to his hair-roughened male flesh. But when she felt him shudder with the surge of desire coursing through him and she realized his hard arousal was nestled against her soft lower belly, her need for him was overwhelming. She had to cling to him for support.

"Why don't we get into bed before we both collapse right here on the floor?" he asked, guiding her toward his big king-size bed.

When she pulled back the comforter and lay down, she watched T.J. reach into the drawer of the nightstand to remove a small foil packet. After he tucked it under his pillow, he stretched out beside her and took her back into his arms.

"You are without a doubt the most exciting woman I've ever known," he said, lowering his head to kiss her with a passion that left her feeling light-headed.

Before she could tell T.J. she had similar thoughts about him, he slid his hand from her hip down to her knee, then back up along the inside of her thigh, rendering her completely speechless. Shivers of excitement coursed through her when he touched her with a feather-light caress, then parted her to stroke the tiny nub of intense sensation within.

Needing to touch him just as he was touching her, Heather moved her hand from his side. When she found his rigid length, his groan was deep and filled with pure male pleasure. "Sweetheart…if you keep doing that…we're both going to be mighty…disappointed," he said, sounding as if he was extremely short of breath.

"I want you, T.J.," she whispered. He tested her readiness for him with gentle strokes that were driving her wild. She wasn't sure how much more she could take without going insane. "Now!"

"I want to be inside of you, too," he said as he reached beneath his pillow for the foil packet.

When he arranged their protection, he took her back in his arms. Nudging her knees apart, he rose above her. Heather's eyes locked with his as she reached down to guide him into her. As he slowly made them one, she savored the exquisite sensations of being completely filled with him.

"You feel so damned good." She watched him close his eyes for a moment before he opened them again and smiled. "I need to love you now, Heather."

"P-please."

He slowly rocked against her and with each thrust of his body into hers, the thrilling tension within her built. The connection she felt with T.J. was unlike anything she had ever experienced with anyone. Though she'd tried to ignore it, that connection had been there from the beginning. It might have frightened her with its intensity if she'd been able to think. But all she could do was feel his body surrounding hers and the mind-blowing friction carrying them toward the pinnacle of fulfillment.

All too soon Heather felt the tightening deep in her lower body reached a crescendo, then set her free as wave after wave of pleasure coursed through her. Holding on to T.J. to keep from being swept away, she felt him surge into her one final time. Groaning, he rested his head against her shoulder and joined her in the satisfaction of sweet release.

Heather held his body to hers as she cherished the unbroken connection between them. That's when she knew for certain they were truly one—one heart and one soul.

Panic began to fill her. Had she done the unthinkable and fallen for T.J.?

After getting to know him, he had turned out to be entirely different from the man she'd first thought him to be. He was kind, caring and the most considerate man she had ever met. And her heart was telling her that she could trust him. When he told her that he would never do anything to cause her or Seth any kind of harm, one look in his eyes left no doubt that he was completely sincere. But it wasn't always that easy. Sometimes causing someone emotional pain was unintentional and unavoidable.

"Are you all right, sweetheart?" he asked, rolling to her side.

She nodded. "That was…"

Her voice trailed off as she stared at him. The caring she detected in his incredible hazel eyes was breathtaking. If she'd had any last traces of doubt about what she felt for T.J., the look in his eyes would have melted them. She *was* falling for him and it scared her as little else could.

"Incredible," he finished for her, unaware of her inner turmoil. Holding her close, he gave her a kiss so tender it brought tears to her eyes. "You're amazing, Heather."

She wanted to tell him what a remarkable man he was, how much she appreciated all he had done for her, but she hadn't yet fully come to terms with her feelings. If she hadn't already fallen in love with him, she was extremely close.

"That was wonderful," she said, meaning it. "But I really need to go back to the bedroom I'm sharing with Seth."

Smiling, he nodded. "I understand, sweetheart." When he got up from the bed, he didn't seem the least self-conscious as he retrieved their clothes from the floor and handed hers to her. "I'll walk you down the hall," he said, pulling on his jeans.

When she put her clothes on and started for the door, T.J. put his arm around her waist and held her against him as they walked to the room where her son was sleeping.

"You never did tell me what you wanted to talk about," she commented.

Stopping at the door, he reached out to tuck an errant strand of hair behind her ear. "It can wait until morning." He cupped her face with his palms and gave her a kiss that caused her toes to curl into the thick hall carpet. "Sleep well, Heather."

As she stepped into the room and closed the door behind her, she doubted she would get any sleep. She had a lot to think about and some decisions to make concerning the Circle W and how much she should tell him about her situation.

And if she didn't have enough on her plate, she had just added one more: the fact that she was falling hopelessly in love with T. J. Malloy.

When T.J. returned to his house after meeting with the furnace repairman out at the Circle W, he found the note he'd left Heather earlier that morning lying on the kitchen counter, indicating that she was still asleep. Smiling, he walked down the hall to his office. After putting the mail he had picked up from her mailbox on his desk to give to her later, he climbed the stairs and opened the door to her room to check on her and Seth.

"Hi!" Seth said, standing up in the play yard. Grinning, he motioned toward the bed across the room. "Mom-mom seep."

T.J. put his finger to his lips to silence the toddler and stepped into the room to pick up Seth and carry him out into the hall so he didn't disturb Heather. "How are you this morning, partner?"

The child babbled something that T.J. didn't even pretend to understand.

"How would you like to have breakfast with me while we let your mom get some rest?" he asked, carrying Seth downstairs to the kitchen. "Would you like to help me whip up a skillet full of scrambled eggs?"

"Otay," Seth said, nodding.

T.J. was thankful the kid liked eggs. Aside from making sandwiches, scrambling eggs and popping bread into the toaster were the only culinary skills T.J. possessed.

Gathering all the things he would need, T.J. pulled one of the kitchen chairs over to the counter, stood Seth in the seat and got a mixing bowl down from one of the cabinets. "You can help me scramble the eggs and milk together," he said, earning a big grin from the little boy. "But when it comes time to cook them on the stove, all you can do is watch. Understand?"

"Otay," Seth agreed.

Once he had the eggs cracked and put into the bowl, T.J. added a little milk to make them fluffy and smooth, then reached for a wire whisk. He handed it to Seth, then held the bowl and guided the toddler's hand in a circular motion.

It was going to take twice as long to get the eggs scrambled enough to put in the skillet, but T.J. wouldn't have missed the smile on Seth's face for anything in the world. The kid was having a ton of fun, and as far as T.J. was concerned, that made it worth the delay.

"Why didn't you wake me?" Heather asked, hurrying into the room. T.J. turned in time to see her glance at the clock. "I've missed the appointment with the furnace repairman."

"Don't worry about it," T.J. said, as he continued to help Seth mix the eggs. "I met him over at your place just a little while ago and he said the furnace needed a new motor, but that was the only damage. I told him to go ahead and repair it." He shrugged. "The only drawback is, the furnace is so old, he's going to have to order the replacement motor."

"Thank you, I appreciate your thoughtfulness, but you should have woke me up so I could meet with him," she said, setting her purse on the island. "It's my problem to take care of. Not yours."

He should have known she would take his trying to be helpful the wrong way. He'd thought that after the amazing connection they had made the night before, she might be more willing to let him help her. But he should have realized that letting go of her fierce pride was going to be a hard thing for her to do.

"You needed to rest," he said, turning back to see how Seth was doing with the scrambled eggs. "And you told me yesterday that you hoped the furnace could be repaired. All I did was tell the guy what you would have told him."

She sighed. "Did he say how soon the new motor will get here?"

"He told me that because of the holiday tomorrow, it won't be in until the first part of next week." Glancing over his shoulder at her, he added, "Looks like you're going to be extending your stay here." He smiled. "And that doesn't bother me one bit, sweetheart."

She rubbed her temples with both hands. "I can't take advantage of you like that."

"Believe me, I don't mind," T.J. assured her. "You've seen how big this house is. Most of the time, I rattle around in it like a lone bb in an empty boxcar."

"Then why did you build something this big?" she asked, frowning.

"I liked the design and I had the money," he said, shrugging.

He decided because she wasn't in the best of moods to wait until after breakfast to explain that his family spent New Year's Eve at his place every year. Which would lead to him telling her about his family descending on them tonight like a swarm of locusts. She might throw a plate of eggs at him for not mentioning it sooner.

"I suppose that's as good a reason as any," she commented.

Looking into the bowl, T.J. smiled at Seth. "Looks like the eggs are ready to go in the skillet, partner." Lifting the boy down from the chair, T.J. moved the bowl and the chair closer to the stove, but made sure the toddler was well away from any danger. "Ready to watch me cook the eggs?"

"Mom-mom, me hep," Seth said happily when T.J. lifted the toddler back onto the chair.

"I see that." Heather walked over to peer at the skillet. "I thought you said you didn't know how to do anything in the kitchen but make sandwiches."

"Eggs and sandwiches are it," he said, smiling at the most beautiful woman in the world.

After last night, he knew he was a goner. He had never felt a connection as strong or as right as the one he and Heather had shared, nor had he ever felt closer to a child than he did to Seth.

His heart pounded hard against his ribs. Was he really thinking long-term? Was he ready for that?

"Do you want me to take over?" she asked.

"Nope." Thankful for the interruption to his unexpected thoughts, he smiled as he looked at Seth. "We have this, don't we, partner?"

Grinning, Seth nodded and jabbered something that Heather seemed to understand.

"Would you like for me to set the table?" she asked.

"That's sounds like a winner." T.J. leaned over to give her a quick kiss. "And if you're of a mind to, a cup of coffee would be nice. I don't know why, but I woke up tired this morning," he teased. "I wonder why?"

Her cheeks colored a pretty pink. "I'm not going to dignify that with an answer," she said with a smile as she turned to set the table.

While he and Seth finished cooking the eggs, Heather made toast. By the time they sat down to eat, T.J. had a fairly good glimpse of what his life could be if he made things more permanent with Heather. Was that what he wanted?

It certainly wasn't unpleasant. Doing things with Seth—teaching him things—was pretty awesome. And just thinking about making love to Heather each night and waking up each morning with her in his arms had his body reacting in a very predictable way. But an instant family was a lot of responsibility.

He'd lain awake most of the night thinking about what he wanted and he still didn't have any firm answers. On one hand it scared the living hell out of him to make that kind of commitment—to be responsible for someone besides just himself. What if he came up lacking? What if he failed them in some way?

Other than Hank being his foster father during his time at the Last Chance Ranch, T.J. had never had a father. And he really hadn't had an example of what a husband was supposed to be. He'd watched his brothers as they learned what their wives expected of them, but that was only at family get-togethers. It might be different in their daily lives.

One thing that he didn't have to worry about was the financial aspect of being in a relationship. Because of wise investments, his grandkids' grandkids would never have to work a day in their lives if they didn't want to. It was being responsible for their emotional well-being that concerned him. He knew he would move heaven and earth to give Heather and Seth everything they could ever need or want. But was he enough to keep them both happy emotionally?

And then there was the problem of what his life would be like without them in it. Yes, it had happened quickly, but at this point, he didn't even want to think about not having them with him. Yet he wasn't sure that what he felt for Heather was love. He couldn't say he had ever loved a woman before. With nothing to compare to his feelings for Heather, how was he supposed to know for sure?

"You look awfully serious all of a sudden," Heather said, wiping Seth's hands after he finished eating. "Is everything all right?"

"Sure." T.J. decided he could give their future more thought later on. Right now, the time had come to warn her about all of his family showing up later that afternoon. "I was just thinking about what I wanted to discuss with you last night."

"Okay, what's on your mind?" She rose from the table to remove their empty plates, rinse them and put them in the dishwasher. "I'm beginning to think this is something you dread telling me and that means I should dread hearing it."

"It's not anything bad," he assured her. "In fact, I'm pretty sure you'll really enjoy yourself." He nodded at Seth. "And I know my little partner is going to have the time of his life."

"What is it?" she asked, looking suspicious.

He checked his watch. "In about five hours, my family is going to start showing up for our annual New Year's Eve party. I was going to ask you to join us, but we kept getting distracted."

Her eyes widened. "I can't impose on your family gathering," she said, shaking her head until her ponytail swung back and forth. "Seth and I have taken advantage of your generosity as it is. We'll go back home. I'm sure we can stay warm enough if I—"

"Like hell," T.J. said, leaving the table to walk over and take her in his arms. "It's supposed to be colder tonight than it was last night. And while we're at it, let's get something straight right now. You haven't taken advantage of me. I want both of you here with me."

"I don't have anything with me that I can wear to a party," she said, looking distressed.

He frowned. "What's wrong with what you have on?"

She gave him a look like she thought he was being overly obtuse. "I'll be in jeans and a shirt while everyone else is—"

"Dressed just like you," he interrupted. "My sisters-in-law are going to be in jeans and sweaters or sweatshirts." He smiled. "Trust me, you'll fit right in, sweetheart." He kissed her until they both gasped for breath. "You and Seth are with me and I want you to meet my family. I'm betting by the time they leave after brunch tomorrow, you'll be wondering why you were so concerned."

Even as he said the words, he knew they were true. They were a part of his life now and meeting his family was the next step toward making it permanent.

When his brothers and sisters-in-law arrived late that day, Heather was relieved to see that T.J. had been right. She didn't feel out of place at all. The only awkward moment had been when his brother Nate asked if she had a stallion. When she told him yes, he grinned, wrapped her in a brotherly hug and welcomed her to the zoo. She had wondered what T.J. told them about his and her past run-ins, but whatever he'd said hadn't seemed to make a difference.

In fact, she was really enjoying herself. She had loved spending time in the kitchen with the women as they prepared dinner and snacks for the evening. Having other women to talk to was something she'd missed since moving back to the Circle W.

After graduating high school, she had moved two hours away to go to college, met Seth's father and lost touch with most of her girlfriends. Then, when she came back home to live after her fiancé was killed, she discovered that all of her friends had either moved away or they no longer had anything in common. But sitting in T.J.'s family room, she felt like one of the girls again.

"Heather, how old was your little boy when he started walking?" Bria Rafferty asked as she reached for another handful of homemade trail mix. "I've caught little Hank standing alone without holding on to anything several times, but he hasn't tried taking steps yet."

"Seth did the same thing for a few weeks," Heather said, smiling. "Then one day right after he turned eleven months old he just took off." She laughed when Seth ran around the sectional sofa where they were sitting, then ran back toward T.J. and his brothers gathered around the bar. "And he hasn't stopped since."

"He's adorable," Summer McClain commented as she rejoined the group after wiping off her husband's shirt because their daughter missed the burp cloth again. "I love his copper-colored hair. It reminds me of your hair, Taylor. Maybe one day you'll have a little red-haired boy or girl."

"Maybe." Taylor Donaldson smiled as she sipped her glass of ginger ale. "He really is a very sweet little boy, and so cute, Heather."

"Thank you," Heather answered, her chest swelling with pride.

When T.J. walked over to the couch with Seth perched atop his shoulders, Summer smiled. "T.J., you seem to be having fun this evening."

Heather looked around at a couple of the brothers, who were making faces as they tried to get the baby girl in Ryder McClain's arms to smile. The others were letting little Hank try on their wide-brimmed hats. "I think all of the men are having a good time with the kids."

"Of course they're having a good time," Bria agreed, laughing. "These guys are all just large children themselves."

"Hey, I resemble that remark," T.J. said, grinning.

"We know," all four women said in unison.

As their laughter died down, Taylor's husband, Lane, walked over to join them. "Are you ready, babe?"

"I suppose so," she said, smiling as she rose to her feet.

"You aren't leaving, are you?" Bria asked.

"Nope," Lane answered, grinning. "Hey, could you sorry excuses for cowboys stop propping up the bar and come over here for a minute," he called to his brothers.

"What's up now, Freud?" Sam asked, walking across the room with his giggling son wearing his hat.

"He's probably going to try to analyze all of us," Nate said, laughing.

"If he hasn't figured out by now that your elevator doesn't go all the way to the top floor, he might as well set fire to that psychology diploma of his," T.J. said dryly.

"So what's up, Lane?" Ryder asked, handing his baby daughter to his wife.

"Taylor and I wanted to let you all know that in a little less than eight months we're going to add another member to the family," Lane said, gazing lovingly at his wife.

"God help us," Ryder said, laughing. "Another little Freud." He stepped forward to shake Lane's hand, then hugged Taylor. "Just a word of advice. Get as much sleep between now and the baby's due date as you can."

"Yeah, after the baby gets here, sleep won't be much more than a fond memory," Sam said, tickling his giggling son.

"You know who to call for babysitting," Nate Rafferty said, raising his beer bottle in salute.

"Yeah, anybody but you," Jaron Lambert said, smiling. The most reserved of the brothers, Heather decided he could be the poster child for the phrase *the strong, silent type*.

Heather continued to watch the genuine joyful response of all the family members to the news of a new baby on the way and she couldn't help but envy them. As boys, the men had been brought together as strangers by the foster care system and sent to the Last Chance Ranch. But because of their shared experience and the memories they made together as adolescents, they had bonded and become a family that was closer than some who were related by blood.

As the evening wore on, Heather and the other women got their children down for the night, then returned to the game room to talk for a while before they turned on T.J.'s huge television to watch the colorful lighted ball drop at midnight in Times Square. Just before the big event, the men wandered over from the bar to join the ladies.

When T.J. sat down beside her on the sofa, he put his arm around her and drew her close. "Are you having a good time?" he whispered close to her ear.

"It's been a very nice evening," she said, smiling. "I love how relaxed and informal it's been. Thank you for including Seth and I in your family party."

With his arm still around her shoulders, he reached out to take her hand in his. "This is the first one of our family New Year's Eve parties that I've really looked forward to seeing the ball drop," he admitted.

"Why?"

"Because that means I get to kiss you," he said, his eyes filled with such promise it robbed her of breath. "And since there's an hour's difference between here and the east coast, I get to kiss you when it's midnight here, as well."

"I have a hard time believing this is the first time you've had a date on New Year's Eve," she said doubtfully.

"It's the first one since the family started ringing in the New Year together," he said, lifting her hand to his mouth to kiss the back of it.

The gesture made her feel warm all over. T.J. hadn't made any attempt to hide their relationship or whatever it was that was going on between them. From the moment his family began to arrive earlier in the day, he had taken every opportunity to show her affection.

"All right, guys," Nate said, standing up. "The ball has started dropping. On your mark, grab your girls... kiss!"

Heather might have laughed at the man's countdown, but T.J.'s mouth immediately covered hers in a kiss that caused her head to spin. When he lifted his head, he smiled.

"Happy New Year, sweetheart. I have a feeling this is going to be the best year ever—for both of us."

Looking into T.J.'s hypnotic hazel eyes, she hoped with all of her heart he was right.

Eight

The next morning, after the family finished the brunch Heather and his sisters-in-law had made, everyone took off to drive back to their ranches and T.J. breathed a sigh of relief as he glanced over to check on Seth, who was playing on the braided rug on the other side of his office desk. He loved his family—loved getting together with them—but for the first time since he'd started hosting the New Year's Eve parties, he was glad to see them leave.

He'd spent a miserable night in the master suite, knowing that the woman he wanted in his bed was just down the hall. Even the cold shower he had suffered through when everyone went upstairs to their rooms hadn't cooled off the burn he had for Heather.

He had asked her to sleep in his room, but she apparently wasn't yet ready for his family to learn the extent of their relationship. He was pretty sure his family had already figured it out, but if Heather wasn't ready for it to be common knowledge that they were sleeping together, he wasn't going to push the issue.

"Did you send one of your men over to tend to my horses or should I go over to feed them and muck out the stalls?" Heather asked, walking into his office.

When she came around his desk, he turned his chair, took her by the hand and pulled her down onto his lap. "I sent Tommy Lee over there a couple of hours ago," T.J. said, nodding. He gave her a peck on the lips. "When he came back he said everything looked fine."

T.J. started to settle his mouth over hers to give her the kiss he knew they both wanted. But Seth chose that moment to get up from where he had been sitting to walk over to them.

"Mom-mom," the little boy whined, rubbing his eyes.

"I think somebody is still tired from having such a big night," she said, picking up Seth. She smiled. "I need to take him upstairs for a nap."

"You want me to carry him up there for you?" T.J. asked, reaching up to stroke the little boy's copper hair.

She shook her head. "You go ahead and finish whatever you were doing. I'll probably only be a few minutes."

T.J. couldn't resist giving both of them a kiss on each of their cheeks. "I'll be right here when you get back."

As he watched Heather carry Seth from the room,

T.J. couldn't stop thinking about how quickly the two of them had become so important to him. From the time he had found them stranded on his side of the creek, all he'd been able to think about were ways to help them, to keep them with him.

He knew of only one way to do that permanently— with a ring, a preacher and a lifetime promise. Was he really thinking about taking that step this soon?

T.J frowned. Watching her with his family last night, he had come to the realization that he loved her—had probably loved her from the moment she stepped out of her car that night in his garage. And he couldn't care more for Seth if the little boy had been his own child. But was he ready to make that commitment? He was almost positive Heather's feelings for him went just as deep. Would she even consider becoming his wife?

He still wasn't sure that he could be everything Heather and Seth needed. But he could for damned sure try.

Right now, though, he just wanted to enjoy having Heather and Seth in his home for a few more days. He could give the future a lot more thought later. He shook his head and reached for his cup of coffee, accidently knocking off the pile of Heather's mail he had placed on his desk the day before. After he'd come home from the Circle W, he had gotten busy and forgotten all about it.

As he scooped up the pieces from the floor an envelope with Final Notice stamped on the front caught his eye. One look at the return address and he had a good idea he knew what it was. The letter had been sent from the county treasurer's office. He would bet every last dime he had that Heather was behind on her real estate taxes.

He placed the unopened envelope on top of the rest of her mail as the revelation sank in. Knowing what a struggle it was for her to keep the Circle W going, he really wasn't all that surprised. What did alarm him was the fact that she might lose the ranch.

He sat back in his desk chair, trying to think of how he could find out what was going on. She was prickly enough about her circumstances that he doubted she'd confide in him on her own. Asking her straight up was out of the question. She would no doubt tell him where to go and how to go about getting there.

But he needed to know what he could do to help her.

A sudden thought had him breathing a sigh of relief as he turned on his laptop. There was one way he could find out what she was up against and not run the risk of pissing her off. Delinquent taxes, court reports and other records were posted on the county's website. All he had to do was go online and check the public records. If, as he suspected, there was a problem, then he would figure out what he could do to help her.

Fifteen minutes later, T.J. closed the browser on his laptop and blew out a frustrated breath. Taxes hadn't been paid on the Circle W property in three years and the ranch was due to be seized by the county the first of next month. It would be put up for auction after that.

Of course, if the debt was satisfied, along with all the penalties and interest charges, Heather could keep the ranch. But he knew for certain she didn't have that kind of money. If she did, she wouldn't have had to sell off some of her brood mares to make ends meet.

He could offer to pay the taxes for her, but hell would freeze over before she'd let him do that. Or he could offer to lend her the money. But he knew her pride wouldn't allow her to go for that option either. So what was he supposed to do?

Sitting back and doing nothing while she lost her ranch wasn't in his DNA. The Circle W had been in her family for generations and should be there for Seth to take over when he came of age. As long as T.J. had breath in his body and the money to rectify the situation, he would see that it was.

He would help first, and ask permission after. He'd had no trouble winning her over to his way of doing things with all her other ranch problems. This one would be no different.

Picking up the letter from the county clerk, he opened his desk drawer, placed the envelope inside, then slid it shut. Heather had already dealt with more than her share of stress the past few days. He wasn't going to give her the notice and add to it. Besides, he already knew how he was going to take care of the matter. And as long as she didn't know about it first, she couldn't stop him. But he had every intention of giving her the security of the ranch being there for Seth.

"You're looking serious again," Heather said, walking back into his office.

"Just pondering the mysteries of the universe," he said, smiling. "Did you get my little partner settled down for a nap?"

She nodded. "He had the time of his life last night, but he's completely worn-out."

Looking down at the pile of her mail minus the upsetting letter, he handed her the bundle. "I forgot to tell you that I picked up your mail yesterday when I went over to meet the furnace repairman."

"Thanks," she said, taking it from him. "I was just thinking that I should drive over to the ranch and pick it up after Seth wakes up."

As he watched her thumb through the envelopes he felt a little guilty about hiding the letter from her, but he was certain she already knew about the situation and he had already made up his mind about handling it for her. Unfortunately, he couldn't put his plans into motion until the first of next week when the courthouse reopened.

"Heather, I have a horse I need to work with," he said, leaving his desk chair to wrap his arms around her. He had one more decision to make and he needed a little alone time to think it through and decide what he was going to do.

Kissing her, his body hardened so fast it left him a little dizzy. It always seemed to be this way with her. He took a deep breath and tried to focus. If he didn't already know what he was going to do before, he did now. But he still needed time to make some plans and the sooner he got started on them the better.

"Why don't you bring Seth out to the arena when he wakes up and I'll give him a real horseback ride?" he suggested.

"He'd love that," she said, smiling.

When he looked into her crystalline blue eyes, the emotion he saw there convinced him that everything was going to work out to his satisfaction. He was not only going to pay her back taxes, but he was also going to take that leap of faith and ask her to become his wife.

When Heather paid the furnace repairman with the last of her reserves and closed the door behind him, she sighed heavily. Her and her son's fate had just been sealed. They were going to be looking for somewhere else to live at the end of the month, but at least they would be warm until then.

"Hossy?" Seth asked, looking at the door.

"You've got a one-track mind, sweetie." Scooping him up into her arms, she kissed his smooth baby-soft cheek. They had only been home a few hours and she already missed T.J. terribly. It seemed Seth did, too. "Maybe we'll see him when he gets back from Stephenville."

Her son looked at the door again before he shook his head. "Hossy," he said stubbornly.

"You're as determined to have your way as T.J. is," she said, laughing.

When she finally got Seth distracted with the barn that mooed when the door was opened, she made a pot of coffee. Fighting tears, she took the local newspaper and started looking at what was available for rent in the area. For one reason or another, she found fault with all of the places in her price range and she was pretty sure she knew why. None of them were the Circle W or the Dusty Diamond.

Propping her elbow on the table, she rested her chin on the heel of her hand. She could understand feeling this way about her own ranch. It was home. But she really hadn't expected to feel that way about the Dusty Diamond. Of course, it didn't take a genius to figure out why she felt so at home there. That's where T.J. was.

Lost in thought, it took a moment for her to realize that someone was knocking on the door. But apparently her son had heard the sound because when she started to get up from the table, he raced past her.

"Hossy! Hossy!" he shouted, turning back to give her a look that was meant to urge her to hurry up and open the door. "Hossy!"

Before she could reach for the knob, the door opened and T.J. walked in to pick up Seth. "Hey there, partner!"

As she watched, her son threw his little arms around T.J.'s neck and hugged him with all the exuberance an almost two-year-old could possess. "Mine hossy!"

Heather laughed. "I really need to work on him learning how to say T.J."

He tickled her son's tummy. "I'm fine with whatever he wants to call me."

The smile T.J. gave her caused her heart to race and when he put his arm around her shoulders and pulled her to him, Heather's chest tightened with emotion. She realized now that she had been wrong in her assumption that no man could love another man's child as much as he would his own. Just seeing T.J. and Seth together was all the proof she needed to dispel that misconception.

"Would you like some coffee?" she asked, needing a moment to shore up her composure.

"That sounds good." Kissing her, his gaze caught hers. "There's something we need to talk over."

"Oh, dear heavens," she said, laughing as she walked over to pour him a cup of coffee. "The last time we went through this, I ended up meeting your family and they were wonderful."

"Yeah, but you have to admit I had good reason to be nervous about that." He grinned as he sat down at the table with Seth in his lap. "Having all of them together in one place is a lot like trying to keep up with what's going on at a wild horse race," he said, referring to the rodeo event where a team of three cowboys attempted to catch, saddle and ride a wild horse.

"There were times it was a bit of a free-for-all," she admitted, setting his coffee on the table in front of him. Smiling as she sat in the chair across from him, she added, "But in a really good way."

As she watched, he started to pick up his coffee mug, but then stopped with it halfway to his mouth. "Looking for somewhere else to live?" he asked, nodding toward the open newspaper still lying on the table.

Heather's cheeks burned with humiliation as she stared at him. There was no sense in trying to be evasive or lying about it. He would eventually find out anyway. But that didn't make her loss any easier to put into words.

"S-Seth and I are…going to be evicted at the first of

next month." She trained her eyes on her tightly clasped hands on the top of the table. "The taxes haven't been paid since my father got sick."

When T.J. set his coffee cup down, he reached out to cover her hands with his and she had to fight to keep her tears in check. Keeping her gaze fixed on their hands, she refused to look at him. Her pride was taking a direct hit as it was, and she didn't think she could stand to see his eyes filled with pity.

"Sweetheart, that's not going to happen," he said gently.

"Yes, it is," she said, nodding. "Just before Christmas I received a notice from the county telling me they were starting the proceedings to seize all of my assets to satisfy the debt."

"Heather, look at me," he commanded. When she looked up, instead of sympathy his hazel eyes were filled with determination. "I'm telling you that you aren't going to lose the Circle W."

Something in his tone and confident expression caused a cold feeling to spread throughout her chest. "How can you be so sure?"

"I didn't intend to tell you like this," he said slowly. "But the other day when I got your mail there was a final notice from the county about the ranch."

"You opened my mail?" she asked as anger began to replace the dread that had filled her.

He shook his head. "I didn't have to."

"Then how—"

"When I noticed the return address, I went online to the county government's website. It's a matter of public record, sweetheart." He gently squeezed her hands with his a moment before he reached into the inside pocket of his jacket to remove some folded papers. Laying them on the table in front of her, he added, "But as of this morning, the debt has been settled and you're no longer in danger of losing your ranch."

She stared at him for endless seconds as his words settled in. Then jerking her hands from beneath his, she jumped to her feet. "You didn't!"

"Yes, I did," he said firmly.

"Have you listened to anything I've told you these past two weeks?" she demanded.

"I've listened to everything," he said, nodding.

"You couldn't have." His calm demeanor infuriated her even more. "If you had, you would know that I don't want anyone—and especially you—feeling sorry for me. I'm not a charity case. I pay my own bills."

"I don't feel sorry for you," he insisted. "This is not charity. I just want to take care of you and Seth and make your lives easier."

"Do you even hear yourself?" She shook her head. "If that isn't pity, I don't know what is."

"M-Mom-mom," Seth said uncertainly, his little chin wobbling as he looked from her to T.J. Their raised voices were upsetting her baby and she walked over to take her son from T.J.

"I'd appreciate it if you would leave now," she said as she hugged Seth close. "You're upsetting my son."

T.J. slowly stood up. "This isn't over, Heather."

"Yes…it is." She took a deep breath to keep her voice from shaking. "You can't always have your way,

T.J. When you care about someone, you have to listen to what they want. But since you didn't, the Circle W and everything here, with the exception of our personal effects, is yours now."

"Like hell," he said angrily. "I paid the back taxes so that you can hang on to this place for Seth, not because I wanted it. I've got my own place. I don't want yours."

"Well, whether you wanted it or not, it's yours." When Seth started to cry, she pointed toward the door. "Now please leave so that I can take care of my son."

"This isn't over," T.J. said angrily.

"Yes, it is."

Walking over to the door, he turned back. "Don't let your stubborn pride do this to us, Heather."

She stiffened her spine and straightened her shoulders. "There is no *us*, T.J. If there had been, you would have discussed what you intended to do with me before the fact, not after you'd already done it."

He looked as if he wanted to say more, but instead he just shook his head, opened the door and left. She heard him rev his truck's engine a moment before gravel spun and the truck sped down the driveway toward the main road.

"Hossy!" Seth cried, reaching his little hand toward the door as if he knew he'd lost his best friend.

"He's gone, sweetie," she finally said, feeling as if her heart had shattered into a million pieces.

"Hossy," Seth repeated as he buried his face in the side of her neck. His tears wet her shirt and, unable to bear her son's distress, she didn't even try to hold back her own tears.

When her son finally cried himself to sleep, she put him in his bed and wandered back into the kitchen to stare at the legal papers T.J. had left on the table. She'd never felt more lonely in her entire life. Not even losing her fiancé and her father so close together, having a baby by herself and struggling to keep the ranch running had left her feeling as desolate as she felt at this moment. Her breath caught on a sob. She knew now beyond a shadow of doubt that her worst fears had just been realized. She and Seth had both fallen hopelessly in love with T.J. and he had broken both of their hearts.

T.J. sat in his man cave with his second bottle of beer, staring at his reflection in the big mirror above the bar. He'd chugged the first beer in one continuous gulp and he just might do the same with the bottle he held now. Why did he have to fall in love with a woman who had more stubborn pride in her little finger than most people had in their whole damned bodies?

Taking a long draw from the bottle in his hand, he had to admit that part of her reaction was his own damned fault. If he hadn't asked her about the rental ads she'd been looking at in the newspaper, he wouldn't have gotten the cart before the horse.

He reached into the front pocket of his jeans and withdrew the small black velvet box he had been carrying around all day. Setting it on the bar, he opened the lid to stare at the three-carat princess-cut diamond engagement ring he had intended to give her when he asked her to be his wife. His intention had been to ask her to marry him first, then give her the document for the paid taxes as an engagement present.

"Way to go, jackass," he muttered to the man staring back at him from the mirror. "You just might have screwed up any chance you had with her."

Restless, he snapped the lid on the box shut, then got up to toss the empty beer bottle into the trash can behind the bar. Wandering into the kitchen, he found his housekeeper, Theresa, standing at the counter cutting up vegetables for his dinner.

"I hope that whatever you're making freezes well," he said, walking over to look out the French doors leading to his patio. "I'm not hungry and probably won't be eating supper."

"You don't look like you feel well, T.J.," she said with concern in her eyes. "Is everything all right?"

He shrugged. "Things have been better."

"Is there anything I can do to help?" she asked.

"Not unless you can turn back time a few hours," he admitted.

"Sorry," she said, shaking her head. "But it might help if you wait a couple of days before you go talk to the young lady and tell her you're sorry for whatever you've done."

"How did you—"

"I've seen that same look on more than one young cowboy's face when he's done something to anger his woman," she said wisely. "So tell me about this young lady who's stolen your heart."

For the next half hour, T.J. told the older woman

about Heather and Seth and what he had done to fall out of his woman's good graces.

When he finished, she nodded. "You're right. You really messed up. Big-time. But I don't think all is lost."

"You don't?"

"No." She smiled. "As long as you're willing to give her a little time to calm down, I think she'll realize that you meant well, even if you did do something that you knew deep down she was going to take offense to."

"That's it?" he asked incredulously. "That's all I have to do?"

"Well, that and be willing to do a fair amount of groveling," Theresa said, laughing as she put the casserole she had been making into the oven.

"Thanks, Theresa," he said, kissing her wrinkled cheek.

She laughed. "Just remember our little talk the next time I hit you up for a raise."

"Will do," he said, smiling for the first time since he'd left Heather's.

As he walked back into the man cave, T.J. felt more hopeful. He just had to wait the few days Theresa had suggested before he went over to try to talk things through with Heather.

The way he saw it, he had one shot left. He loved her and Seth more than life itself and now that he'd figured that out, he wasn't about to do anything else that might screw up things. Even if he had to wear out the knees on a pair of jeans, he was going to beg Heather to understand and accept that he had only had the best of intentions.

The rest of his life depended on it.

Nine

Heather sniffed back tears as she finished packing the rest of the kitchen items into a carton, then taped it shut. She only had a few more of Seth's clothes and hers to pack and they would be ready to finish loading the small trailer she had rented.

Looking around, her breath hitched on a sob. The Circle W had always been home and she couldn't believe that when she drove away later that afternoon, she would never again be able to walk through the house where she had grown up. Nor would she be able to take Seth fishing along the creek bank or watch him ride his first horse around the feed lot.

But as much as not being able to do those things bothered her, it was never again seeing the man she loved that filled her with sorrow—a pain deeper than she could have ever imagined. She realized that she should have handled the situation a little differently when he'd confessed what he'd done. But why couldn't T.J. understand that by choosing not to talk to her about what he wanted to do, he had cut her out of the decisions about her own family's ranch? He'd made her feel ashamed that she had been unable to do more to save her legacy. He had completely missed, or possibly ignored, her need to be independent and prove herself capable of providing for herself and her son.

"Mom-mom, hossy?" Seth asked, walking into the room.

It tore her apart every time her little boy asked about T.J. She had failed to protect her son from becoming emotionally attached to T.J. and in the end he was suffering as much, if not more, heartache than she was. She was an adult and could understand the choices she had to make. But Seth was too young to realize what had happened.

"No, sweetie," she said, picking him up. "We won't be seeing T.J. anymore."

She had no sooner made the statement than the back door opened and the man in question walked right in. Of course, she supposed he could do that now. After all, he owned the place.

"Good morning," he said, smiling.

Seth immediately held out his arms and leaned toward T.J. for him to hold him. "Hossy!"

"How's my partner doing today?" T.J. asked, smiling. He gave Heather a questioning look as if to ask if he could hold her son.

Not wanting to make the situation any more stressful for Seth, she nodded. Her son immediately wrapped his arms around T.J.'s neck and held on to him as if he was a lifeline. It made her feel worse than ever.

"In a way, I'm glad you stopped by," she said, walking over to the counter for the large envelope with his name on it. Handing it to him, she added, "It will save me having to send you the keys to all of the buildings, as well as the papers you'll need for transferring ownership of the horses and the deed to the property."

"Where are you going to go?" he asked. His expression gave nothing away as to what he might be thinking.

"I thought we might go up to Oklahoma," she answered. "I heard on the news there are several job openings in the Tulsa area."

He looked so good in his black Western-cut suit jacket, white oxford cloth shirt and dark blue jeans, it brought tears to her eyes. She turned away to keep him from seeing her pain.

"There are a few things we need to get settled before you go," he said, pulling out one of the chairs at the table.

"Everything you'll need is in the envelope," she answered. Noticing that Seth had laid his head on T.J.'s shoulder and gone to sleep, she reached for him. "I'll put him in the play yard."

"I'll do it," T.J. said, standing to walk into the living room where she had set up the portable bed. "You've already got Seth's bed taken apart and put into the trailer?" he asked when he returned.

She nodded. "All I have left are a few boxes and the play yard to put in the trunk of my car."

"I'll carry them out for you when we get ready to leave." He motioned toward the chair he had pulled out from the table. "Sit down. There's something I need to tell you."

"I can't imagine there's anything left to say."

He gave her an indulgent smile. "Will you please sit, Heather?"

Sighing, she walked over and sat down in the chair. It was clear he wasn't going to tell her what he thought needed saying until she did as he asked.

"There's something you need to know about me," he said, leaning back against the counter. He folded his arms across his wide chest and casually crossed his legs at the ankles. "It might help you see my side of things and explain my need to take care of you and Seth."

"I don't see how—"

He held up one hand to stop her. "Just hear me out."

"All right."

"My mom was a single mother," he said, meeting her gaze head-on. "I know now how hard she struggled to work, pay bills and take care of me. And believe me, she did a hell of a job and made a lot of sacrifices just to keep me from finding out that we didn't have it as good as everyone else." He shook his head. "When I look back, I realize now that all those times she said she wasn't all that hungry were really times that she was leaving the food for me so that I had plenty to eat."

She watched a shadow of sadness briefly cross his

handsome face and knew that what he was about to tell her next was something that had caused him a lot of emotional pain.

"What happened?" she asked softly.

"My mom and I both got the flu when I was ten," he said, giving her a meaningful look. "There wasn't enough money for both of us to see a doctor, so she made sure I was taken care of, but she neglected herself. I got better. She didn't. She died of pneumonia a week or so later."

"Oh, T.J., I'm so sorry," she said, realizing why he had been so insistent that she stay at the Dusty Diamond when he learned that she had the flu.

"Me, too," he said gruffly. He seemed to take a sudden interest in the tops of his expensive alligator-skin boots. Then he raised his head to look directly at her. "The night I found you and Seth stranded by the flooded-out road, I made a vow that I wouldn't let the same thing happen to your son."

"I—I had no idea," she stammered.

"Just like my mom, you didn't have anyone to take care of you. You didn't have anyone to see that you got better." He shrugged. "I couldn't walk away from that."

"I don't know what to say." She was completely stunned.

"I didn't want you to know," he said, shaking his head. "I didn't insist on taking care of you so that you would feel sorry about me losing my mom when I was ten years old." He pointed toward the hall. "I did it for that little boy in there. I didn't want him going through life without his mother."

Tears filled her eyes. How could she have ever thought that T.J. wouldn't love her son as much as his own father would have?

"Is that when you went into the foster system? After your mom passed away?" she asked.

"No, I was sent to live with my great-grandmother," he said, shaking his head. "But she was elderly and didn't have the energy to chase a preadolescent boy who had a knack for getting himself into trouble every time he turned around." He reached up to rub the back of his neck as if he was trying to decide how much to tell her. "I was put into the system when I was fourteen. She passed away a couple of months later."

"You were in trouble?" she asked, completely shocked.

He nodded. "I fell in with a bad crowd and landed in juvenile detention more than once for vandalism. For whatever reason, my case worker decided that I was a candidate for this new foster home run by an ex-rodeo champion."

"That's why it was called the Last Chance Ranch?" she asked.

"Yup, and it was the best thing that ever happened to me," he said, smiling fondly. "Hank Calvert made me face the anger I'd felt at losing my mom. He made me realize that instead of blaming everyone else for it, I should accept that's just the way things go sometimes. He also believed in me and after a while, I started believing in myself."

"So all of your brothers were in trouble, too?" she asked, marveling at the men they had all become.

"We were all hell-raisers," he said, laughing. "But with Hank Calvert's help, we all straightened up our acts and became honest, upstanding citizens."

"I would have never guessed," she admitted.

"He saw to it that we all went to college, too." T.J. grinned. "You could never tell it by looking at me, but I'm more than just a rodeo cowboy who won a couple of world championship belt buckles. I graduated from Texas State with a master's degree in business."

"Hank sounds like a wonderful man," she said, meaning it. "Sam and Bria's son is named after him, isn't he?"

"Yes." T.J. shoved away from the counter and walked over to her. Kneeling down in front of her, he took her hands in his. "Heather, I know you think I was being high-handed when I paid your taxes, but I only wanted to do something that would help relieve the stress I know you've been under for far too long." He kissed each one of her palms. "I don't ever want to see callouses on these hands again from where you've had to work like three men just to keep this ranch running."

"I don't think you have to worry." His kind words were causing her heart to break all over again. "Remember, you own the Circle W now."

"Sweetheart, did you bother looking at the documents I left here the other day after I paid the taxes?" he asked, smiling.

She shook her head. "No. I didn't have the heart."

"I never said I bought the ranch for back taxes," he said, his tone indulgent. "I said I paid the taxes. And if you had bothered to look at those papers, you would have seen that I paid them in your name."

"But it wasn't your responsibility," she insisted. "It was my debt. I couldn't pay them and I—"

"I understand that, sweetheart," he said, kissing her. "But I was going to give you the papers as a gift after I asked you something."

A bubble of hope began to form inside of her, but she tried to tamp it down. "What were you going to ask me, T.J.?"

As she watched, he pulled a small black velvet box from his jacket pocket. "I was going to ask you if you would consider making me the happiest man on earth by becoming my wife. Then I had planned to give you those papers as an engagement present." He flipped open the box. Resting inside was one of the biggest diamonds she had ever seen.

"Oh, my God!" she said, covering her mouth with her hand. "I never... I mean, I didn't know... I never dreamed..." She let her voice trail off when she realized she wasn't capable of coherent speech.

"I love you, Heather," he said, his expression quite serious. "I will always love you. And if you'll let me, I'd like to take care of you for the rest of my life."

Tears trickled down her cheeks as she looked at the man she loved with all her heart. How could she have been so stubborn and let her pride get in the way of the happiness she could have with this wonderful man?

"T.J., I'm so...sorry," she said haltingly. "I know I'm stubborn and—"

"You don't have to apologize, sweetheart." He shook

his head. "I knew you weren't going to be overly happy about it. But if my plan to give the paid tax receipt to you as an engagement present had worked out, it would have probably saved both of us a lot of heartache."

When a fresh wave of tears began to roll down her cheeks, he set the ring box on the table, stood up and lifted her from the chair. Then he sat down with her on his lap. "I hope like hell those are happy tears," he said, holding her close.

"Y-yes," she said, putting her arms around his neck. "I love you with all my heart, T.J."

"Yes, they're happy tears or yes, you'll marry me?" he asked, grinning like he already knew.

"B-both."

"Thank God!" He removed the ring from the box to slip it on her finger. He kissed her then and the warmth of his love lit the darkest corners of her soul. When he lifted his head to gaze at her with more love shining in his eyes than she would ever deserve, he smiled. "There's one more thing that I would like to ask you."

"What's that?" she asked, wiping the tears from her cheeks.

"If you don't mind, I'd like to adopt Seth," he said seriously. "I love that little boy and I swear I'll be the best dad I can possibly be."

"I'd like that," she said, knowing he would be a wonderful father to her son.

T.J. smiled. "He's actually another reason I wanted to pay the taxes on this place. I wanted to make things easier for you, but I also wanted to make sure it was here for him when he gets old enough to take it over.

It's been in your family for generations and I didn't want him to lose that."

"Thank you," she whispered as more tears threatened.

They were silent for several minutes as they enjoyed being in each other's arms again.

"When do you want to get married, Heather?" He chuckled. "And please don't make this a long engagement. I want to start our lives together as soon as possible."

"How does Valentine's Day sound?" she asked, happy to give him his way on this particular issue.

"Better than the Fourth of July, but still further off than I'd like," he said, kissing her again.

Happier than she ever dreamed it was possible to be, she smiled. "Since I'm going to be your wife, could I ask you something I've been wondering about?"

"Sweetheart, you can ask me anything," he answered.

"What does T.J. stand for?"

Groaning, he rested his forehead against hers. "I guess you'll find out anyway when we get our marriage license."

"It can't be that bad," she said, shaking her head.

"Believe me, it's not that good," he replied.

She cupped his lean cheek with her palm as she gazed into his eyes. "Why don't you tell me and let me decide?"

"Tobias Jerome," he said, rolling his eyes. "I don't know what my mom was thinking when she hung that name on an innocent little baby."

"It's not bad at all," she said, wondering why he didn't like it.

"Do I look like a Toby or a Jerry?" he asked, raising one dark eyebrow.

"Well, not really," she admitted. "You do look more like a T.J. than either one of those two names.

"That's why when we have kids there won't be any of them named Tobias Jerome," he said, laughing.

"How many children do you want?" she asked, loving the idea of Seth having a brother or sister and no longer worried at all that T.J. wouldn't have enough love for all his children, biological or adopted.

"I've got a big house with lots of bedrooms," he said, grinning. "How does seven sound?"

"We'll revisit that subject later," she said, laughing.

His expression turned serious. "I love you, Heather."

"And I love you, T.J. With every breath I take."

Epilogue

"Well, we're down to two unmarried brothers now," T.J. said as he and his brothers stood at the bar in his man cave-turned-family room, celebrating his and Heather's wedding.

They had decided on a small intimate ceremony, with only his family in attendance, and that suited him just fine. The fewer guests they had, the sooner he could whisk Heather away for their honeymoon.

"Who do you think will be next?" Sam asked.

"Well, it isn't going to be me," Nate said. "I'm about ready to swear off women for good."

"And if you believe that, I've got some prime real estate in Death Valley to sell you," Ryder said, laughing.

T.J. looked lovingly over at his beautiful wife, who was talking with his sisters-in-law and Bria's sister,

Mariah. "That's what I said, Nate. And look at me now. I couldn't be happier."

"Yeah, but Heather is a great woman," Nate retorted. "She's not as unreasonable as you once thought and she's definitely not as unreasonable as most women."

T.J. couldn't help but smile. None of his brothers had any idea about what he and Heather had worked through to get to where they were now. And he wasn't going to enlighten them.

"It could be Jaron," Lane suggested.

When Jaron didn't protest immediately, they all turned to catch him staring at Mariah again.

"What?" he asked, clearly unaware of Lane's comment.

"We were just speculating on whether you or Nate will be the next to take a trip down the aisle," Lane said, grinning.

Jaron shook his head. "You better bet on Nate," he said emphatically. "If you're betting on me, you'll lose."

"I've got Nate," T.J. said, plunking down a hundred-dollar bill on top of the bar.

"Who's going to hold the pot this time?" Ryder asked.

"I'll do it," Sam said.

As T.J. watched his brothers each place their bets on who they thought would be the next to get married, Seth ran up and threw his arms around T.J.'s leg. "Mine daddy!"

Laughing, T.J. picked up his son. He and Heather had told Seth that T.J. would be adopting him and would be his daddy. That was all it had taken for the kid to abandon calling T.J. *Hossy* and to start calling him *Daddy*.

While the brothers continued to speculate on Nate's and Jaron's prospects, T.J. carried Seth over to the woman they both loved with all their hearts.

"I don't know about you, but I'm about ready to start our honeymoon," he whispered in her ear.

Her smile robbed him of breath. "Me, too."

"Did you get Seth's things together for Sam and Bria to watch him while we're gone?" T.J. asked, setting Seth on his feet to go play with his new cousin, little Hank.

Heather nodded. "Bria had Sam put Seth's suitcase and car seat in their car just before the ceremony."

T.J. pulled her close for a kiss that left them both breathless. "Then let's get out of here, sweetheart."

"You never did tell me where we're going," she said, giving him a smile that had him burning to get her alone. "Can you at least tell me which direction it's in?"

"Does it matter?" he asked, laughing.

She shook her head and when she put her hand in his, T.J. felt like the luckiest man alive.

"Whatever way you go, cowboy, I'll be right by your side."

"I love you, Mrs. Malloy," he said, kissing her again.

She lightly touched his cheek. "And I love you, T.J. With all my heart."

* * * * *

*If you loved this story
don't miss the other novels in*
USA TODAY *bestselling author Kathie DeNosky's*
THE GOOD, THE BAD AND THE TEXAN,
*a series about six foster brothers from the
Last Chance Ranch!*

*HIS MARRIAGE TO REMEMBER
A BABY BETWEEN FRIENDS
YOUR RANCH...OR MINE?*

All available now from Harlequin Desire!

COMING NEXT MONTH FROM

HARLEQUIN Desire

Available February 3, 2015

#2353 HER FORBIDDEN COWBOY
Moonlight Beach Bachelors • by Charlene Sands
When his late wife's younger sister needs a place to heal after being jilted at the altar, country-and-western star Zane Williams offers comfort at his beachfront mansion. But when he takes her in his arms, they enter forbidden territory...

#2354 HIS LOST AND FOUND FAMILY
Texas Cattleman's Club: After the Storm
by Sarah M. Anderson
Tracking down his estranged wife to their hometown hospital, entrepreneur Jake Holt discovers she's lost her memory—and had his baby. Will their renewed love stand the test when she remembers what drove them apart?

#2355 THE BLACKSTONE HEIR
Billionaires and Babies • by Dani Wade
Mill owner Jacob Blackstone is all business; bartender KC Gatlin goes with the flow. But her baby secret is about to shake things up as these two very different people come together for their child's future...and their own.

#2356 THIRTY DAYS TO WIN HIS WIFE
Brides and Belles • by Andrea Laurence
Thinking twice after a reckless Vegas elopement, two best friends find their divorce plans derailed by a surprise pregnancy. Will a relationship trial run prove they might be perfect partners, after all?

#2357 THE TEXAN'S ROYAL M.D.
Duchess Diaries • by Merline Lovelace
When a sexy doctor from a royal bloodline saves the nephew of a Texas billionaire, she loses her heart in the process. But secrets from her past may keep her from the man she loves...

#2358 TERMS OF A TEXAS MARRIAGE
by Lauren Canan
The fine print of a hundred-year-old land lease will dictate Shea Hardin's fate: she must marry a bully or lose it all. But what happens when she falls for her fake husband...hard?

YOU CAN FIND MORE INFORMATION ON UPCOMING HARLEQUIN® TITLES, FREE EXCERPTS AND MORE AT WWW.HARLEQUIN.COM.

HDCNM0115

REQUEST YOUR FREE BOOKS!
2 FREE NOVELS PLUS 2 FREE GIFTS!

HARLEQUIN® *Desire*

ALWAYS POWERFUL, PASSIONATE AND PROVOCATIVE

YES! Please send me 2 FREE Harlequin Desire® novels and my 2 FREE gifts (gifts are worth about $10). After receiving them, if I don't wish to receive any more books, I can return the shipping statement marked "cancel." If I don't cancel, I will receive 6 brand-new novels every month and be billed just $4.55 per book in the U.S. or $4.99 per book in Canada. That's a savings of at least 13% off the cover price! It's quite a bargain! Shipping and handling is just 50¢ per book in the U.S. and 75¢ per book in Canada.* I understand that accepting the 2 free books and gifts places me under no obligation to buy anything. I can always return a shipment and cancel at any time. Even if I never buy another book, the two free books and gifts are mine to keep forever.

225/326 HDN F4ZC

Name	(PLEASE PRINT)

Address		Apt. #

City	State/Prov.	Zip/Postal Code

Signature (if under 18, a parent or guardian must sign)

Mail to the **Harlequin® Reader Service:**
IN U.S.A.: P.O. Box 1867, Buffalo, NY 14240-1867
IN CANADA: P.O. Box 609, Fort Erie, Ontario L2A 5X3

Want to try two free books from another line?
Call 1-800-873-8635 or visit www.ReaderService.com.

* Terms and prices subject to change without notice. Prices do not include applicable taxes. Sales tax applicable in N.Y. Canadian residents will be charged applicable taxes. Offer not valid in Quebec. This offer is limited to one order per household. Not valid for current subscribers to Harlequin Desire books. All orders subject to credit approval. Credit or debit balances in a customer's account(s) may be offset by any other outstanding balance owed by or to the customer. Please allow 4 to 6 weeks for delivery. Offer available while quantities last.

Your Privacy—The Harlequin® Reader Service is committed to protecting your privacy. Our Privacy Policy is available online at www.ReaderService.com or upon request from the Harlequin Reader Service.

We make a portion of our mailing list available to reputable third parties that offer products we believe may interest you. If you prefer that we not exchange your name with third parties, or if you wish to clarify or modify your communication preferences, please visit us at www.ReaderService.com/consumerschoice or write to us at Harlequin Reader Service Preference Service, P.O. Box 9062, Buffalo, NY 14269. Include your complete name and address.

HD13R

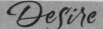
Here's a sneak peek at the next
TEXAS CATTLEMAN'S CLUB:
AFTER THE STORM *installment,*
HIS LOST AND FOUND FAMILY
by *Sarah M. Anderson*

*Separated and on the verge of divorce, Jake Holt is
determined to confront his wife. But when he arrives
in Royal, Texas, he finds that Skye has been keeping
secrets...*

Jake had spent the past four years pointedly not caring
about what his family was doing. They'd wanted him to
put the family above his wife. Nothing had been more
important to him than Skye.

He was not staying in Royal long. Just enough to get
Skye back on her feet and figure out where they stood.

Just then, the baby made a little hiccup-sigh noise that
pulled at his heartstrings.

Jake's brother picked the baby up so smoothly that
Jake was jealous.

"Grace, honey—this is your daddy," Keaton said as he
rubbed her back. Then, to Jake, he added, "You ready?"

Not really—but Jake wasn't going to admit that to
Keaton. He tried to cradle his arms in the right way. Then
Keaton laid the baby in them.

The world seemed to tilt off its axis as Jake looked
down into his daughter's eyes. They were a pale blue—

just like her mother's. Up close now, he could see that Grace had wispy hairs on her head that were so white and fine they were almost see-through.

She didn't start bawling, which he took as a good sign. Instead, she waved her tiny hands around, so of course he had to offer her one of his fingers. When she latched on to it, he felt lost and yet *not* lost at the same time.

He was responsible for this little girl from this moment until the day he drew his last breath. The weight of it hit him so hard that if he hadn't already been sitting, his knees would have buckled.

This was his daughter. He and Skye had created this little person.

God, he wished Skye was here with him. That things between them had been different. That he'd been different.

But he couldn't change the past, not when his present—and his future—was gripping his little finger with surprising strength.

Don't miss what happens next in
HIS LOST AND FOUND FAMILY
by Sarah M. Anderson!

Available February 2015,
wherever Harlequin® Desire books and ebooks are sold.

HDEXPO115